CW00871333

Jason Williamson

Happy Days

Amphetamine Sulphate
2020

Published by Amphetamine Sulphate

PO Box 41087

Austin, Texas 78704

Third UK printing

ISBN 978-0-9991825-6-7

Contents

Pat and the Boulevard

The sound of the indicator messed with the music a bit. She missed whole chunks of her favourite bits in certain tunes because she'd always start the album from track one and it would always be the same journey, the same route, each day. The indicator went off at roughly the same time because of this, distorting the same bits on the same songs depending on how mad the traffic was. Obviously that differed from album to album but Pat liked to cane a long player if it was good enough. She'd rinse an album for at least five weeks. And it was funny in the gridlock on a rush hour you know, just sat there amongst all the other fucking square traps. It didn't matter what car you fucking had, did it? They all looked the same in the lined stationary pit of rush hour. That Series 5 just looked like any other cube with arches. It didn't differ from the other plain wagons, wasn't exclusive anymore. The gridlock became its Krypton - sandpaper to its shine, powerless. Pinning it down and sucking its desire rating straight out of the exhaust pipe until it lay humiliated, screaming at the sky as it turned on its owner in a blind fury, like a switched dog. Ripping into them as they sit motionless, useless. Their minds pummeled by pride, ego, by leather interior and the myth of individualism. If you sat the driver down with the driver of a cheaper car, what would you see and how would that feel? Would you see two clearly different people? Would it become clear that a more expensive car sure did elevate a person? And even if you did notice a stark contrast between them, so what? Confidence was a joke really, and Pat assumed that's what the difference would be, let's face it. People always seemed happier behind 'things,' didn't they? If you had lots of desirable shit, if you had big muscles, then the world loved you. It was easy street. What was confidence built on? The modern concept of confidence was like cheap structural groundwork's, drunk on the breath of tasteful ownership. The basic trickery of consumerism, the absurdity of possessions, bought the moment to a conclusion for Pat. You just bought what you liked if you had the cash and if you didn't you then had to make a sizeable compromise and feel like a mild cunt. But even in that, it bought no comfortable logic really. We were slim on options; it was stark, regardless of wealth, or not, as the case may be. The whole thing was a complete bag of shit, wasn't it? Absolute shit.

This idea that we were all already in Hell too, that was another thing that pissed her off. The idea that life was this fucking Hell and how that was a notion not only more plausible but accepted too, unlike the more fantastical concept that greeted you after death. This was clearly a well-trodden discussion but it didn't make it any easier to process, it was a fucking piss-take, wasn't it. It was an ultra *dog's existence* that attached a firing squad to almost everything you tried to elevate. Pat resented the scenery out on the sides of each road she drove down. The caged poverty and roaming loners that she went by at whatever mph; screaming at nothing or at whoever happened to pass them.

Pat hated the skinny black trees that gave the parks the preferred hotspots for the doggers in the area. She loathed the fucking Dogging group on Facebook, it fucking ruined it all. It wasn't a fucking model aeroplane get together, you know. It was Sex! Not some fucking coach trip to Yarmouth. Some of the members would post awful fucking messages:

Looks like good weather this Friday folks, so let's make this one a real gudden! See ya down there!

It depressed Pat. She'd get down to the location looking for a large measure of carnalism and a lot of the time it was like watching ya Uncle Calvin waving his little cock about after watching too many Carry On films. Pat wanted hard fucking fun, not that shit. The blokes were fat fuckers too. Who wants that? Pat wanted at least a bit of muscle, for fuck's sake, a fucking slither please! She'd looked after herself because it suited the idea of good sex, of the fuck. I mean she did think sometimes that perhaps it wasn't that important to look physically attractive in the way the State requires; you know, the way they *want* you to look. But that would pass and she would adhere to her strict exercise routine. But these people? Jesus, not an ounce of muscle between any of them and how's that any good? These fucking men just turn up after a few in the pub and think they can fuck anyone. They do it so badly too, like really fucking badly. Most of them are really unfit and the noises are comical, like sitting next to a heavy smoker on the train who's eating a fucking Dominos or something. Coughs and chest tugs on an abnormal level, slurps and all that fucking dross. This wasn't dogging, this was a toilet poke during the reception at the social club, between two people who didn't know what they were doing and why they were doing it. Fuck all that.

'So, he's been OK today. A loose poo at lunch time and then one at dinner.'

'What? One at tea time too?'

'No, tea time was fine this morning. But obviously we don't give them hot drinks haha, just juice.'

'I meant dinner time, you know, 'tea time,' 'dinner time.''

'Sorry? Dinner time?'

'No, what I meant was, we call 'dinner time' 'tea time,' that was all.'

'Oh. Haha. Oh OK yes. Yes, one in the afternoon as well.'

'Both of them loose then?'

'Yes.'

'Right. I'm gunna get him checked out with the doctor at some point.'

'Yes do so, but you know it could be anything. Wheat is just the tip of the iceberg, isn't it, when it comes to allergies.'

'Yea, so I'm finding out.'

Pat took Clive from Sharna's arms and picked his boots up from the wooden shelving next to the entrance.

'OK then. See you Friday.'

Sharna handed her Clive's freshly baked bread, which caused Clive to scream out loud.

'BREAD! BREAAAAAD!'

Clive was on the verge of talking. His words were beginning to form, but it was still mainly noises and unsettling sobs, so she didn't feel too guilty not engaging a lot whilst driving home; and plus she thought it was great exposing him to good music, actual music, as he sit there looking on in amazement at all around him, chomping on his bread. Pat's dad was never moved by music, really. Just the obvious bollocks the masses bought into and never questioned, so she was exposed to nothing of any merit and resented him for not elevating her a tad; music was everything.

The rush hour blockage meant the drive home was around 45 minutes both ways and such an oppressive part of the day. Like a job, a real job where you started, clock-watched, hated everything about it (with the exception of Clive) and finished. The sights were horrible, the landscape scathed and moaned. Hills and flyovers came in and out, the tangled heads of traffic lights and panicked workers scrambling for the near touch of home.

After tea it was a bath for Clive and then bed. Arse got in around six so it wasn't too bad in the evenings. Pat had been married to Arse for nearly a decade. His real name was Henry, but she nicknamed him Arse because he nearly always farted. Henry didn't mind, so it stuck.

'I don't know why that fucking dickhead from the group keeps insisting we go round his house for a foursome.'

Arse fell into the kitchen and threw his phone on the side and put his bag next to it.

'Evening. Who? Fucking Donald Pleasance? What's he been saying now?'

'Evening. Haha yea. He looks like him, doesn't he. What's he been saying? Oh the fucking Usual. Twat. Wanting us to go round his place for a foursome thing. His wife's fucking minging too.'

'He's no oil painting either, to be fair.'

'Shall we leave the group, you think?'

'No! It's the only one about.'

'Why don't we start looking at fixed orgies, ya know, house parties?'

'Because they are usually shit. Worse than dogging! I've started to think it's because we're English. If you watch any type of porn, any, it's always the UK stuff that's shit, isn't it. I don't think it can shrug off its past, can it. Not in a porn sense, but in a cultural sense, you know. 'No Sex Please, We're British' and all that. Most UK porn is like watching fucking Benny Hill innit.'

'You're thinking about this too much. The reality is far different I think. Well, kind of. You fancy chips? I take it big man's in bed?'

'Yea, he went down 20 minutes ago. Chips? I'll go get em if you wanna have a shower or something, just keep ya ear out for him, will ya.'

Pat pulled up outside the Cod Daddy. It was an odd name for a chip shop. Like some incorrect take on a famous film for irony's sake, or whatever, and plus it sounded a bit wrong, a bit pervy.'

'Hey, Pat.'

'Hi, Sol.'

The queue was massive but at least it was popular. A quiet chip shop on a Friday night wouldn't be good.

'Hiya, you.'

Halfway up the queue stood Donald Pleasance. His actual name was Rene, a short, stocky and round-faced man in his late '40s.

'Oh hiya, Rene. You alright?'

'Yea, not bad. Getting some chips.'

'Well, obviously.'

'Not so, my dear. I mean, I could be getting fried chicken! Hahaha.'

'Yea, but odds-on you'd be getting chips, wouldn't you? I mean I wouldn't feel happy putting money on you buying chicken now, haha.'

Rene moved down and parked himself next to Pat. Pat looked bemused.

'Oh, it's alright, Pat, dear. I've ordered.'

'Oh, OK.'

'You get my message?'

'Yea, Arse said he'd received something. I try not to go on Facebook too much in the day mate, it's a fucking void, isn't it.'

'Well, the offer's there if you fancy it. I know we do, hur hur.'

'Oh, OK. I'll have a look at the message when I get back then. Left my phone at home.'

Rene moved into Pat's ear.

'That's a good little girl, haha.'

Pat stepped back a little.

'OK, mate. OK.'

Arse was pinching Pat's chips after shovelling his down in less than nine minutes.

'They're mine!'

'Alright, alright! So you reckon we should, then?'

'Fuck it, why not. Rene's alright, he's good at licking cunt.'

'His missus is fucking minging, though.'

'Look, just take some base with you. I'll get Lol Party to look after Clive.'

Lol Party was Arse's sister. Named as such because she was a miserable bastard who always sucked the life out of everything.

'Hahaha. The Lol Party won't have that. She'll not take the boy for two nights I know, and plus, fuck whizz. I can't do it anymore.'

'She will, and believe me, take some whizz. At least then you won't have to fuck fishface, will ya, and 48 hours is plenty to consume and come down. I mean, we'll only be there for, at the most, eight hours.'

Rene's wife, Hanna leaned against the fridge, as Arse did the same against the kitchen units that faced opposite. He was completely twatted. Hanna wasn't into it at all.

'So when did you take it, then?'

'Oh fucking hell, about an hour ago.'

'Surely you'd have known, though. I mean, no cunt gets a hard on doing that, do they?'

Arse started playing air guitar to absolutely no music.

'They do Hanna, they do. Just that initial stage innit, you know, the rush bit.'

'Well, fuck me, and I wish you would by the way, but if this is the rush bit what's the fucking leveling out look like, Henry? Finger me, come on, fuck me with ya hand, then.'

Arse went into a kind of air guitar solo whilst just sticking his tongue out at Hanna. He clearly hadn't heard her. Hanna just stared at him, expressionless.

'This the sugar pot?'

Arse was holding a clay milk jug in his hand as if it were the skull of Yorick to his whizz-infested Hamlet. Hanna looked at him with a mixture of disbelief and boredom as she slowly started to fall inwards. She felt ugly, exposed, bored and sick of all this shit. She kept thinking about disconnecting, leaving Rene and all this sex stuff, for good. It just littered his every thought. His face had turned in on itself of late, hardened and twisted with the many sexual obsessions that festered. The various strains of *lust* he had summoned within himself had him pinned to the kitchen chipboard, for fuck's sake.

There was more surely, more than this, the smell of other people's bollocks and fannys. There is surely more than strangers, who then become invaders, heavy handed and disgusting.

'You wanna fag, Munter?'

Arse was now motionless with the exception of his head, which was nodding in time to the house music coming through the speakers. Hanna fixed her eyes on him.

'What did you just call me? Munter?'

As fucked as Arse was he quickly realised what he'd just said. He tried to conceal it under the guise of intoxication.

'No, Hanna. I didn't call you Munter.'

'Yes, you fucking did.'

'I didn't.'

'Is that what you think about me then? Think I'm ugly? Is that why ya not fucking me?'

'No, no. Don't be daft, mate. Look, come on then. Let's fucking do it!!!'

Hanna turned her lip up and folded her arms.

'Fuck off.'

Pat was laid on the sofa in the living room, partly anyway. Her head and shoulders were hanging from the sofa arm and Rene's head was between her legs. The back of his neck and shoulders looked like some kind of giant hairy oyster shell. His ability however to make her squirm in absolute pleasure was second to none. She bucked at his face gently, pressing his head harder onto her vagina. Arse walked slowly into the room still playing air guitar. Hanna followed him. She was by now partially naked and grinning.

'Oi, I fucked her, babe. Fucking shagged her. On fucking base too!'

Pat turned her head a little to look at them both. Arse looked so fucking pathetic, and in that moment, so not the person she wanted to be with. Hanna sat down on the couch just behind Arse. She looked like she'd had some base as well.

'Did they fuck?' Pat thought. 'He looks wasted. No fucking way. Why? Why say that? Fucking twat.'

She kept pressing Rene's head deep into her, gyrating, holding the position; then back again. Arse was now in the far corner of the living room near the giant TV, kind of watching them. He was still playing air guitar and sticking his tongue out at Hanna, like a dog suffering in intense heat. Hanna slowly got on her hands and knees and motioned towards the end of the sofa where Pat was hanging. She started kissing the top of Pat's head moving slowly down to her forehead. Pat pushed her away subtly.

'Not now, Hanna. I'm fuc …'

'OK, OK. Chill out, Pat. It's OK.'

Pat looked at Hanna and thought she'd really connected with her for a minute. Like Hanna understood the kissing wasn't what she wanted. Hanna had put the energy of the sex before her ego. Pat turned back to look at Arse.

'Fuck him, fuck the twat,' she thought. 'Fuckin idiot.'

By now he had lost interest in the air guitar thing and was biting bits off a peach he'd pulled out of his pocket, trying to spit them at Rene's arse. Rene, who had been pretty much out of sight for most of this, pulled up from Pat momentarily to see what was going on. He clocked Arse throwing the bits of fruit, smiled, and returned to Pat's vagina. Rene then started blindly trying to position his arsehole in line with the aim of the flying fruit. Pat tried to go with this for a minute but the spell had been broken.

'Oh, for fuck's sake, you pair. This is fucking nonsense.'

Arse stopped in mid throw and looked at Pat.

'I'm bored. Why are you letting this cunt fuck you with his tongue? He's minging.'

Inter Town

'How's that photocopying shop goin, you got?'

'It's a high end printers, graphics studio. We don't photocopy.'

'It's a fucking paper shop though, innit?'

'No, a paper shop is what people refer to a newsagents as.'

'Yea, but you know what I mean.'

'Not really.'

Paul finally got the barman's attention.

'What ales you got in the fridge, mate?'

'All local, The Funnels End, Chepney's Spasm and Big Josh.'

'What's that Big Josh like?'

'Good. 7.6, nice and neat.'

'I'll take one please. Jerry, what do you want?'

(To the barman) 'Pint of Heineken, mate.'

'It's off. Stella?'

'Oh for fuck's sake no. That stuff's shit. I'll have that Josh thing then. Can I get two? And a pint glass?'

'Yep.'

Jerry moved over to let two blokes in and Paul circled around said blokes with a tray carrying the drinks. They both returned back to the table near the front entrance where Stephen sat. It was Friday, 9.53pm. Late February.

'Jerry, you got that thingy?'

'Yea, but it's shit by the way, three for a ton, keeps you awake. I like it. I know you're a crackhead, mind.'

'Haha. Can I buy one off ya? My bloke's coming down in half hour, so I'll have a load.'

'What you getting?'

'80 quid jobs, I'll just whack that kiddy shit you got in two lines.'

'Look at hard man.'

'Hardly, I'm wanking with tweezers on gear, hahahhaha. There is nothing fucking glamorous about me, you poor cunt, you can fucking forget leg-over, mate, I just finger her. All these wankers bragging about fucking on gear, nah, it don't happen.'

'Steve the tweezer wanker, hahahaha.'

'Yea, least I'm honest though, you poor cunts boring me shitless with hard man porkies, fuck off, pure snore innit.'

'Aye (pointing to Paul), he got wound up cos I called his arty-farty shop a photocopiers.'

'No Jerry, it just wasn't funny.'

'Look, haha.'

'You wanna watch Paul, mate, he's fucking proper Jerold, he'll have ya.'

'What with? A graphic design? Hahahaha.'

Stephen goes to the toilet and locks himself into a cubicle and pulls out the bag of coke Jerry gave him. He then pulls out his wallet and takes a card out. He lunges the corner of the card into the bag and gathers a sizeable amount on it, carefully bringing it back out of the bag and up to his nose hole. He repeats this operation three times, flushing the toilet only on the last action in order to get the lot properly up his nostril cavity.

He carefully packs all the objects away into their rightful places. He checks his phone, puts it on top of the toilet roll holder and pulls his shirt up slowly, gathering and holding it in place under his chin. He then pulls his trousers down to just above the knees and slowly shuffles back towards the end of the toilet. He leans over and rests his back against the wall of the cubicle and starts stroking his balls. He reaches over to his phone and takes a photo of himself in this position. He then sits on the toilet, with the lid down and takes another photo of his chest, stomach and cock area, tops of his thighs, et cetera, making sure to tense all where possible for maximum photo effect. Last month he did this and tensed so hard his feet slipped on the moat of piss that surrounds the toilet base and it made a right racket, he nearly got caught, or so he thought, so he's careful not to make any noise this time. He views the photos then turns round and rests one knee on the toilet lid and bends over to take another of the side of his arse, legs and lower chest. He looks at this one the most then deletes the other two. Eventually he dresses himself, opens the door, washes his hands and joins his friends.

'What you been doing? Wanking?'

'I told ya I can't get a hard-on on this shit. Nah, dropped me card in the fucking loo.'

'Bout right with the wages you get then.'

'Haha, yea. Minimum wage with a shit allowance, hahaha.'

'Fuckin Paul piping up, you posh cunt.'

'Oh fuck me! A man decides to use his head and all of sudden he becomes a posh cunt, well I never.'

'Aye, Butterball's just come in when you was in the loo.'

'His missus with him?'

'Nah, just him and that twat he works with, that little short twat who wears combats with Trickers.'

'Trickers with combats, you don't do that.'

'Useless, no accounting for taste.'

'Butterball's missus must be pissed to be honest.'

'What permanently? He's a packet of cunts.'

'He's fucking useless. Got the sack from ours cos he said he was allergic to fucking furniture polish, wouldn't do any cleaning.'

'Cunt, mate.'

'We off anywhere else? This is a bit bloke heavy, where's the slot?'

'We got seats ere, fuck that.'

'What are you? 80?'

'Let's go to thingy, fucking Bar One.'

'It's shit, bouncer's a twat.'

'It's full of slot.'

'You leaving that, Paul? Chuck it ere.'

BAR ONE

'Stet at that.'

'Who Posh Spice? She's alright.'

'No No No, her mate, look.'

'What? Oh! Rank Spice!'

'Hahahahahahahahahaha.'

'Where's Stephen?'

'Loo.'

'Cunt's wanking again, ain't he? He looked fucked walking down here.'

'Nailed half that bag you gave him, hasn't he. He wants to watch out, man u'll have a fucking stroke. What do you reckon to that new Oasis album then?'

'Fuckin shit.'

'*I can see a liar, sitting by the fire*? Does that little cunt think we're daft? It's shit. I mean that 'Little James' tune. Fucking shit.'

'Not a bad melody though.'

'What melody? Fucking Honda?'

'Hahhahahhahahhahhah.'

'What you doin?'

(Paul is sticking a 50p into his bag of drugs)

'Fuck this, I ain't queuing up in the toilet.'

Paul nails the bump fairly quickly and puts everything back in its rightful place, before reaching for his drink.

'Thing is, with Oasis, going back to what you was saying, is that they were fabricated by Tony Blair, although it was John Major's Conservative cabinet that masterminded the plot and that kinda got passed down to Blair when he won in '97; and it was him who made them mega famous. By '97 they were everywhere, right?'

'Oh, fuck off!'

'No, serious! I'm being serious ere. The Stone Roses right, they left such a hole in the side of this fucking country's youth culture when they stopped and fell out of sight that it unnerved the powers that be. I mean you had club culture, but that was fading a bit, the kind of passive attitude that came with ecstasy was beginning to lose its glow; and the Government knew that they had to act, to keep us down with something, so they invented Oasis because they saw a potential enterprise in the lad culture that the Stone Roses arguably invented.'

'Oh, fuck off, Paul. How did John Fuckin Major invent them? Who wrote 'Live Forever'? Fucking 'Columbia', and what about the Mondays and all those bands? Don't be a poor bastard. You think too much, mate.'

'Yea, but look where thinking got me Jerold, mate.'

'What? Stood next to a useless cunt like me in a pub with no fucking women looking ya? Hahaha.'

'Look, the Mondays helped for sure, but they were fucked weren't they, from the off? Just twatted all the time and it showed massively. People kinda didn't take them so seriously, plus they were imploding proper by then and in my opinion they were out there musically, it was far more advanced than the Roses stuff, it was different and so the crowd, although they embraced them at the same time, they kept them in a little corner, if you know what I mean. It was the Stone Roses, they were the main draw and the country was ready to follow, ya know.'

'Hahahahaha, fuck me, ya mad mate.'

'Look, Major and Blair both knew of the potential properties that drug culture had in swaying public mood, or at least a large part of it and that in itself was kinda perfect for helping to implement Thatcher's vision of the free market; of greed, of the destruction of communal existence, an ideology both Major and Blair believed in. They looked to the crime issues going on in Colombia with the rise of the drug barons and the product they were wreaking havoc with (pulls out his coke) à la fuckin sniff innit.'

'Mate, ya tapped.'

'John Major looked to replicate in the crashing rubble of the baggy scene a group as powerful as the Roses, and with the right group he thought it could usher in a new wave of drug consumption to sedate the masses. And that product was Cocaine. By inventing a band that was more about the 'self,' about defeatism, about commercialism but with a similar stylised edge, a front if you like, that was similar to the Roses. I'm telling you now, both Major and Blair thought a group with this mentality would complement the nature of coke, the total 'me me me me' psychological grip it has on the user, and as such the result could potentially coerce tens of thousands of their fans into state conformity if the group took off. It was a gamble, of course, but a gamble that fucking paid out.'

Jerry had by now lost interest and was staring at the table next to them both.

'Look at that cunt.'

Stephen had wandered out of the loos and knocked someone's drink over on the table across from theirs. Both Jerry and Paul watched as he apologised to the couple on the table whilst trying to pick the pieces of glass up from the floor. Stephen's trousers weren't properly done up and his arse was sticking out. The bar's manager came over and told him not to bother with the broken glass on the floor. Stephen stood dazed over the mess whilst the manager swept it up with a brush and pan.

'Steve! Over here! The fuck are you doing? Where you been?'

Stephen shuffled over and leaned into Jerry as if he was doing an aside in 'Othello' or something. He was totally battered.

'Loo, innit. Missus called me, fucking barking at me. I told her I was out n' that. Oh fuck me, shall I get them another drink?'

'You alright?'

'Yea, twatted. Your gear is alright innit, fuck me.'

'Pull ya jeans up, mate, haha. You been wanking?'

'You wish, you fat poor cunt and don't drink my beer. I'm meeting Richard outside, more gear.'

'You don't need anymore.'

'Yes, I do.'

Stephen walked out the bar apologising again to the couple whose drink he knocked over.

'Is he buying them another one then?'

'Dunno.'

'Anyway, so John Ma-'

'Oh shut up Paul, fucking hell. I'm not listening to that bollocks all night.'

'Hahaha, I got a point though aye, fucking stinks all that shit.'

'Well it depends if you're obsessed, and you are.'

Paul pulls his bag out again for another bump.

14 minutes pass.

'Where's that cunt?'

'Rich is ere with his 80 quid gear, I told ya.'

'He's off his fucking head innie? Just fucking stupid.'

21 minutes pass.

'He's not coming back is he?'

Stephen was in Richard's car.

'Drop me here mate, ta.'

'You alright?'

'Yea, why?'

'You look fucking twatted, mate'

'Sez the drug dealer.'

'No Stephen, no not really. I'm driving round selling drugs to people, it's my job. I don't view that block of sniff in my pocket as fucking cornflakes that make me tell jokes. Look at ya! Hahaha.'

'I'm alright.'

'Later then.'

'Laterzzz.'

Stephen walked into the off-licence on Sale Road. He skirted the aisles looking over at the till area to see if the place had any porn mags on the stands. In the end he bought a copy of the Sport and the Evening Owl because too many people were in the queue and obviously he didn't want to look like a cunt buying porn, which pissed him off to be honest because the guy behind the counter knew he was in here for porn magazines and gave him a teasing smirk. He was so off his face that he just sat in the bus stop opposite the off-licence, rolling badly made roll-ups that were all really wet at the end because he was so off his tits, looking at the back pages of the papers he bought for any soft porn shots and especially any local personal ads in the Owl.

'I'll give you my phone if I can fuck you. I've ran out of cash.'

'What, that Nokia? Or you got another?'

'I haven't got another, I'm not a fucking drug dealer.'

'Clearly not. You look like the type who gets fucked on his own shopping. You wanna give me that Nokia for a fuck? They've only just come out, you sure?'

'Let me kiss you again.'

'Alright Tarzan, fucking hell, calm down.'

Stephen kissed her passionately, so passionately you would have thought he'd fallen in love with her. What turned him on the most was that she told him she'd just gone through two blokes in a flat above the off-licence where he'd bought the papers from, and that really got him going. The taxi driver had taken them down a little country lane out of town. It was completely secluded and Stephen got the impression he was getting off on it due to the enthusiasm he clearly had for taking them there. Sadly though, the taxi ride was gunna eat all of his cash, so sex with Janet wasn't going to happen unless the phone deal came off.

'OK, I'll take the phone.'

'Can you take us back, mate?'

'Yea, good idea. Keep your phone.'

'You smell of babies.'

'That's because I've got one. You?'

'No.'

The drive back swapped in-and-out of desperation for more drugs, how to get them, and astounding disbelief at the situation in hand. Roads became clearer as dawn broke and the cab's heating hummed, cradling Steve's rattling frame and recovering visual focus from the chaos of intoxication and its blind alleys, its dictatorial absolution. Janet chatted with the cab driver. Steve thought about touching her again but didn't. It made it different now, the baby thing; the tops of her brown hold ups didn't look the same and her energy made him feel ashamed. The cab driver dropped her near the end of Sale Road. She didn't say goodbye.

'Where do you wanna go, mate?'

'Mulston Drive, please. Can you stop at a petrol station too, mate?'

Lifenet

Dipper hated Astras. I mean, he didn't *hate* them but, you know, they were shit, weren't they, on a par with the Ford models really; although he couldn't fault Ford's solid engines and he hadn't met anyone yet who moaned about owning one with a shit engine. Just the obvious gripes about the look of the fucking things and the fact that Henry Ford more or less invented mass fucking production. So, when Daniel pulled up next to the pub across from the café, Dipper muttered a 'for fuck's sake,' coupled with a smirk, stood on his fag and pulled out a quick pace across the road to get into the passenger side.

'Ya alright.'

'Sound. Ya always ere, ain't you?'

'Yea, a bit. No computer at home innit.'

'Yea, but ya in ere for hours, mate. Fuck for?'

'Uploading music on my page, listening back to it, mate. Busy shit, hahaha.'

'Do I look like I just started primary school? Hahaha! You're floating porn and necking this, aint ya? Haha. Here take it quick …'

Daniel handed him a badly folded piece of packed A4 paper and Dipper put a few notes into the gear stick gaiter.

'Ta. And no, mate, porn ain't allowed. Look at the place! How am I shuffling skin in there!'

'Where there's a will there's a way, Dipper. Ta, it's OK too, this.'

'Nice one. Cheers. Hey, all this business you're doing and ya still in this fucking Astra mate! What ya doing?'

'Showboats always sink, Dipper. I like the fresh air, me.'

'Haha.'

It was late June and whatever poor excuse for a summer this country got each year usually intensified around this period. The road was busy with traffic and the Saturday shoppers walking the long stretch out of the city towards the outer districts gave it a bit of colour. Dipper studied Daniel's expression as he pulled off. Dealers, the ones that didn't use anyway, always had a wise air about them, but Dipper knew this was bollocks. He came to the conclusion it was a front to make their product seem better. You know, a philosophical cunt seems a lot more believable and trustworthy than a basic thick cunt that could smack you instantly should he or she want to. Underneath they were defiantly all dark bastards, across the board.

Nothing beat the pick up though. The part where you were beer buzzed and rattling with nervous expectation as you waited for your order. The impulsive decision to abandon whatever rational sense that still remained deep within his rattling cage also gave Dipper a feeling of empowerment and for a short collection of minutes it was as if he was free from the absolute lot, the whole thing. The off-licence next to Lifenet was run by the same people, an Albanian family, and from what Dipper could gather, a few of their mates too, so he knew he'd be OK buying beer and going back into the café.

They were good people and Dipper was always polite. Manners are good currency.

'You OK with this, mate?'

Dipper held the two cans up, desk height to the bloke in the chair at the front of the café. He sat behind a small table with two monitors facing him. He never ever spoke to Dipper, just nodded constantly. Dipper put this down to him not having a great command of the English language, that or he just thought Dipper was a sad bastard who spent to much time in the internet café and thus didn't deserve the beauty of verbal communication. The bloke nodded his approval for the illicit bag of booze to be consumed on the unlicensed premises and Dipper shot to his seat. Lifenet was found half way up the main road out of the city. It boasted 12 monitors, each with its own booth and cost £1.50 for 30 minutes, three pound for an hour and so forth. Dipper used the place as a bedroom but without the sleeping and stale sweat.

He liked to do cocaine whilst uploading the hard work him and his band mate Cato did. 'Cato' was actually a nickname for his mate, Lee. Dipper nicknamed him as such after the Pink Panther movie character, because he liked to playfully beat him up on arrival at the studio where they'd book sessions in. It was a laugh. The only difference between Lee and Burt Kwouk's character, however, was that Lee wouldn't hide anywhere in waiting. He'd just be sat motionless in the chair next to his monitor and Dipper would casually walk in and throw a mic at him or something. Lee would attempt to laugh but it sounded like a murmur. He was a quiet bloke, broken mostly, animated only when the right amount of beer had floated into his system. Dipper would usually fuck him off once the session had ended. He couldn't afford to get him gear too and plus it tainted the relationship if there was too much going on. Occasionally he'd get the drugs in at the studio and they'd go for it, but that was at the start of the month when Dip got paid, so apart from that he wouldn't bother. It would be nice to do it with him all the time, he thought. They'd record intensely for up to four hours per session, anything longer than that and it wasn't working as far as Dipper was concerned. He would pace around the small basement unit, calmly shooting orders at Lee in between looking for lighters and playing back takes, slagging off whatever band was rehearsing next door. They were always shit.

Dipper placed his two cans on the side next to the monitor and being careful not to leave anything else on the desk, he went to the toilet to get started on his drugs. The toilet at the back of the café was always clean, but on its bright pink walls grew a nervousness that mixed in beautifully with the 'well, I can't sink any lower'-type feeling that bit into Dipper's shoulders. It reminded him of the bad choices he constantly regarded as good ones. It made him feel like he wasn't supposed to see stuff like this anymore, like he should of graduated from this standard of fucking living a long time ago. He felt bullied as the wall's grinning mouth spluttered at him:

Look at you, dippy boy! Oh deary me! The rock star! The failed fucking idiot sniffing shit drugs into your fucking tiny mind because it helps with the delusion! What happened, dippy boy?!

'Fuck off! You're a wall! And stop spitting into my fucking drugs, you pink cunt.'

The toilet roll was like somebody had carefully unwound it and separated each layer of paper that formed each perforated padded square, just to make it last longer. It disintegrated like a cheap wafer when he wiped the rim to go for a shit after waxing two big lines. Dipper preferred to sit on the actual toilet rim and did not, as the majority of people would, use the toilet seat. He was under the impression it was cleaner that way, because the plastic seat probably housed a fucking league of rank arse and poo germs. Freda, his partner, just stared at him for what seemed like an eternity when he explained this to her one morning. He could never figure out why.

Dipper re-emerged unloaded/loaded and strolled down the narrow aisle to his booth. He slid the CD into the player and waited for the icon on the desktop. He placed the headphones over his head, clicked on the flashing icon and … boom! His world was transformed, all became clear. The moth-bitten plate he had wrapped around his neck couldn't touch anything now. Dip glided in and out of the demo's beauty like a mermaid through a forest of fucking seaweed. The bloke at the front desk looked at him. Dipper returned the look and then nodded, it was a moment of connection, of respect, he thought, and all was good, all was proper as he opened his first can and played the tune again. Dipper rolled a fag and played the tune once more. It was too much, he couldn't believe how fucking proper it was. He felt terrifically proper. He paused the tune, made sure he didn't leave anything valuable on the desk and went out the front of the café for a smoke.

The alleyway received him, gently pulling him into its narrow area. He leaned against its wall and looked at the tree that stood to his right and bang in front of the café. The tree loomed over and gave Dipper's immediate area an almost continental feel, it was beautiful and he wished he had one of those new iPod things so he could batter that new tune even more. Then he thought about Marvin from the label and wondered what he would think. Then he remembered what he had to do and it spoilt things a bit, to be honest. He just wanted to fuck about and what made it worse was that he'd forgotten what Cato said about attaching an mp3 to an email. He couldn't text him because Cato never had any credit. He had a premature crash; he stood on his fag and went back in to the café.

'Man, you just put the tune on Desktop, yea, and then press attach in the email, which should bring it up and that's it.'

Dipper was on the phone to Marvin, a fucking late '60s beatnik-looking wannabe who worked for the label in London.

'Yea, but I've done that, Marvin. It's fucking not working.'

'Haha, look man, keep trying. If not, when you down here again?'

'I'm seeing Freda Thursday actually, my girlfriend. Fuck. Yea, I could come down before I train it to the south of the river?'

'Man, you got a girl down here? Man, that's sweet. Fuck yea! We're above the jazz club on Creek Street, yea? Man, we'll be there after 7pm, cos you work, right? So call me, yea. You're a *head* up there, man. I know your tune is gunna rock.'

'Yea, I'll get the 5ish train. Yea, it's good, mate. It suits that tune you gave me, you know.'

'Man, if this remix comes off, we'll release it!'

'Yea, fucking hell. Yea, mate.'

'Thursday, man.'

'Yea, mate. See ya then Marvin ...'

Dipper rolled another fag and shook the bottom of his nearly emptied can.

'Head? What the fuck's a *head*? Stupid London cunt.'

Dip felt closed in. He suddenly realised he was absolutely bollocks'd. He made sure he had his other gram in his safe pocket before collecting his stuff up and leaving the café. The bloke behind the desk just nodded.

Thursday.

The *Stupidly Records* offices were as Dipper imagined them to be. They teased him with the possibility of success. The walls barked at his ears over the tedious rabble of a coked up Marvin with his Brian Jones hairdo wafting about. The owner of the label, a bloke with a hunch and cocaine intake a man of his age shouldn't have, paced around the area where the music system stood. Behind him on the wall above the speakers was a gigantic montage of popular rock musicians. He shuffled over to Dipper and Marvin.

'You homophobic then, mate?'

Dipper looked a bit stunned.

'What?'

'The 'Bummer' line in this tune. I got a lot of gay friends.'

'No, Richard. It's just an observation, you know. How people talk 'n that, the tune is about how people are.'

'I got a lot of gay friends, mate. Marv said you got a girl down here. She a good girl, mate?'

'Yea, I've got gay friends too, mate. And yea, she's alright, Richard.'

Dipper didn't like Richard. He thought he was a cunt. He felt a tightness hit his throat. He wondered if the cunt had ever sucked a cock, because Dipper had. Fucking London cunt. But that wasn't the point, really. 'Homophobic?' he thought to himself. 'Fuck off.'

'You want another one Dipper, mate?'

'You sure, mate?'

'Yea, no problem, honestly!'

Marvin glanced over at Richard, who had now sat down with his other assistant on the table over from them.

'That OK, Rich?'

Richard nodded.

'So this tune, mate. I thought you were gunna use the *big chorus* in it, you know.'

Dipper's heart sank. He went on the defensive.

'Nah, I didn't like it much, mate. I just looped that first bit and did what I did.'

Marvin racked two up.

'I mean, don't get me wrong, mate, it worked. Fucking funny some of it, hahahaha.'

Dipper just looked at him. He had by now concluded that this visit was not going to get him out that fucking warehouse and into the jacket of stardom. He sunk instantly.

'But I really thought you were gunna use that big chorus.'

'Well, you know, I could have a go at it again.'

'Let me play it for you again, Dip.'

Marvin bounced over to the music system. He put on the original record and all of them immediately started nodding their heads to the wank indie beat, apart from Dipper.

Clueless cunts.

Dipper eyed the mound of gear next to Richard and hated him even more.

'Is she a good girl?'

Cunt. He kept playing that line over and over in his mind.

Dipper seethed as he plucked a ciggy out of Marvin's packet without asking. He had now entered into the 'I'm going, fuck this' mindset. He knew what the score was here.

He'd fucked it. He'd fucked it because this fat old cunt thought he was homophobic and plus he didn't really get the tune anyway. This trendy little studio with its careerist dickheads was an indie mortuary, a dinosaur scratching at its own bones as the meteor ripped through the skies and smashed into the ocean. He'd made it off his own back and he'd never listened to anyone because he didn't have to, because he knew! And now he'd made it all the way to the offices of fucking Stupidly Records and there they were, just pissing into his mouth and wiping his chin down with a fucking Shed Seven tea towel. What a waste of time.

Freda looked like somebody had put a discus in her mouth. The people on the table next to them must've also nipped home and changed their clothes, Dipper thought.

'You're not supposed to snort it, babe. It's ketamine, babe. You nearly fell over going to the loo.'

Dipper lurched in.

'Yea, but fuck it. I just wanna get …'

'Get what, you twat?. You look fucked, haha.'

'Get my pocket, babe.'

'What do you mean 'get ya pocket?' You get ya pocket! God you are fucking mullered, Dippy. Hahahaha.'

'I got some Coke, babe.'

'Where?

'Pocket.'

'Which one?'

'Left one.'

Freda snuck into his left pocket and pulled out a cigarette packet.

'In here?'

'Yea.'

'Get in!'

'Let's go do some.'

'No, I'll go, then you. We can't both go, it's dead in here, they'll notice.'

'Let me go first then, babe. I'm fucked.'

'Drink some water, ere.'

'Tar.'

Dipper drank the entire bottle of sparkling water Freda had bought. He waited five minutes then went outside to have a fag. He came back in and winked at Freda:

'Feel a bit better.'

'You sure? You look worse.'

Dipper didn't hear her. The toilet was old but clean. The Victorian floor tiles gleamed as he hit the cubicle, locked the door and knelt down over the loo. He wacked a good three lines up and carefully put the bag back. He fell back into the chair as Freda grabbed it out of his hand. She sped to the toilet. Dipper nodded his head in time with George Benson's 'Broadway' as it shot through the speakers on the decking outside in the beer garden. He felt better. The head nodding was a sign he was back in control. He hated ketamine.

'So they didn't like it, then?'

Freda had been to the toilet and bought more drinks. Dipper didn't even notice.

'Nah, said they did, but I know they didn't.'

'Fuck em. Be other times for ya.'

'Yea.'

'Cheer up, then.'

'I'm alright. Just twatted. I'm alright.'

Shop Star

So Long 52 is positioned at the corner of Top Gate in the centre of the city. It's an independent store carrying lots of high-end clothing labels, such as …

Wise Owl

Cone Island

Wee Wee Company

Butcher

Gary Giles

Out Sourced

Darren is arguing with Tunnel, the shop's manager:

'Ya being a fucking rude cat, Tunnel, mate.'

'Heeeeey, Dazbo. Come on, man.'

'My name's fucking Darren, twat. Fucking 'Dazbo,' what's that? I'm not a new line in Haribo's, you twat. The fuck has it got to do with you what I drop? You fucking stand in this shop all day, you cunt. You got fuck all! Fucking shop stars, haha. Look nice, always fucking skint.'

'Yo, Daz. You gotta get out, mate.'

Benchard came from behind Darren and gently put his hand on Darren's left shoulder.

'Come on, mate. You can't be shouting like that. There's customers in here, Daz.'

Darren calmed down.

'I'm going, I'm going.'

Benchard followed Darren out of the shop occasionally looking back at Tunnel who was trying to recompose himself behind the counter, shaking his head slightly and working hard at giving off the impression that he had no idea why Darren kicked off like he did. Of course, this was all for the benefit of Tunnel's new part timer, Rose, a 19 year old law student who seemed quite bemused by it all anyway. Tunnel knew exactly why Darren kicked off, of course he did.

Benchard walked Darren out of the shop and onto the walkway.

'What ya saying, Daz? Ya can't do that shit, mate.'

'Fuck him, mate. You saw it. Fucking giving it the arrogant one n' that, fuck's up with him? I remember that little cunt coming into Boss when he was a fucking no one, no cunt knew him, him and his fucking missus bobbing their heads to the tunes we were playing, fuck off! He's a fucking dickhead, Benchard.'

'Yea, but you got to rise above that shit, mate, put some armour on innit, play them lyrics out, Daz. Tunnel's just a bit basic innit, hahaha. He ain't got no angle, mate, you know that. Come on, what's his angle? He ain't got one, mate.'

Darren looked upwards towards the end of the Strip, and gave off a little smile.

'He's a little cunt, Benchard.'

Benchard motioned back towards the shop entrance.

'I'll see ya about, Daz, mate. I'm at TIN tonight, you down?'

'Dunno, might do. I got Cheese's 30th and I think he wants to go Fat Hippo for a few.'

'It's shit in there, mate! Come TIN!'

'Hahahaha, might do. Might see ya later.'

'Inabit.'

'Later.'

The Strip was named as such because it was the beating heart of the City's pay zone, the center of the Money Pattern; a pattern so exact that when you chose its route you were thrown into a bobsleigh and pelted across, under and around its area, its pay zone, where high fashion shops (now accessible to the lowest form) and vodka bars grabbed at you until you were 'washed' gradually by their slow transformation of your physicality and your internal being. Nothing was too big to for it to handle and the Strip grabbed anyone willing, sucking her or him into the barrage of dense non-fancies. Once snagged the Money Pattern would then fully integrate those chosen with illusions that were perched atop its multiple inside jacket pockets. These were your options, bland output and shiny nothings; absolutely fuck all. The people who hung from its trees were nothing more than current representatives appointed by its guards, as directed by the Money Pattern, and thus distributed along the Strip. Once you were chosen you became very, very special; bound for whatever level of fame fitted your role and above all else, you were branded as 'Cool.' Cool is the enemy of humankind. It is the extracted water from the remote spring lake falling from the side of the highest mountain where you get the really unreachable pure stuff. The lake looks so good, it smells so good and it is completely 'Street' without ever, ever knowing the street. It is totally apart from unattractive realities, totally separated from your cheap loaf because it has never known your cheap loaf; so to be able to acquire the Lake's infinite sexdom is mindblowing for the fresh-faced representatives on the Strip. A bewildered state of ecstasy takes over, an animalism that causes the representative to rip and grab, at the mercy of those that are trying to push away from the shores of the cheap loaf.

'I ain't bothered, ya fuckin' train spotter. If it's not in, I'm not wearing it. I don't care if that's shallow. I don't fucking care if that's like jumping on some fucker else's wagon. What's the point if it's not in? Clothes look shit mostly if they ain't in. They lose their power, just look fucking daft. You look fucking daft innit! HAHAHA!'

'I'm not a train spotter, Cheese. Kiss my arse.'

'No, you kiss my fucking arse, cunto! I mean who's fucking winning 'ere? Look at ya! Ya look like Ken Dodd!'

Cheese and John were sat at the back of the raised section in the Hippo.

'Fuck off with ya Ken Dodd. You lot didn't mind looking like this when it suited ya.'

'Yea, cos that's when it looked good. Now it looks shit dunnit, I mean, no offence, you cunt, hahaha, but ya know what I'm saying, don't you? Boating jackets are shit, John mate, it's done.'

'Oh piss off, Cheesy. Load of bollocks. I'm into it …'

'I hate people who say 'I'm into it' too! Load of shit, John mate. It makes me think they're not, like they are fucking trying too hard.'

'Alright, Karl.'

'Who's Karl?'

'I thought you knew, ya kit! Hahahaha, who's the dickhead now? Who's not into it now?!'

'What are you on about?'

'I meant Karl Lagerfeld, but it went over ya head!'

'Oh, fuck him. That's daft fashion shit. That's not real, is it? It's for rich cunts.'

'Yea, but you spend dough on stuff.'

'Yea, but not like that.'

'Alright you sweaty Caucasians?'

Rohit appears before Cheese and John's table and carefully takes his bag from around his neck and over his shoulder, placing it next to John.

'Alright, Ro? Ow are ya?'

'Better than you pair of basic white cunts, I can tell you that.'

'You do realise, Ro, that 'Caucasian' can mean a whole range of races? It's not just a term for white people.'

‘I don’t care for exacts, John mate, not when I’m addressing a basic white cunt in a boating jacket. You look like Mick Talbot mate, hahahahahhahahha.’

‘Hahahahahhahahhahah.’

‘Hahahahahhaahhahahaha.’

Both Cheese and Rohit throw laughs at each other. John reaches for his drink.

‘I’ve got your thing, Cheesy. I’m meeting Tunnel in 20 minutes, so let’s bash this out. 30 plus the 30 from last month.’

John turns to Ro after placing his drink on a new beermat because Cheesy has virtually nibbled both his and John’s into small saliva ridden pieces. Cheesy watches him do it.

‘What you doing?’

‘Fucking glass slips all over on these tables. You need to stop eating beermats, you fat cunt.’

‘Twat.’

John re-addresses Ro:

‘So lets have a look at this weed then, Ro.’

‘Why? Are you smoking it, Mick? Hahahahahahaha.’

‘No, mate, I just wanted to see if you’d been in the woods again.’

‘The woods? You’ve lost me.’

‘Well that last lot you gave Cheese was just fucking twigs and seeds! Hahahahahaha.’

Ro tries to adapt but his posture stiffens.

'Well, you wouldn't find seeds in a fucking wood, would you, Mick? And if Cheese has any issue with my product, I'm sure he'd tell me.'

'He's only winding you up, Ro.'

'Well, the Caucasian needs to watch out then, Cheese.'

'Er, I am ere you know, and furthermore, how do you think woodland grows, Ro? Hahaha, with seeds!'

Rohit just about manages to grab on to the humour's coat tails.

'I see you two have had a few already then. I'm sure you'll be arseholed later to the point of oblivion. I'm off to spend time with more refined company gentlemen, then head home to the soothing sounds of Miles Davis.'

'I bought 'Porgy and Bess' last week, Ro. Fucking brilliant.'

'What? You did?'

'Well yea, you cheeky B.'

'Have you heard this, John? Cheese the Jazz master! Hahahaha. Well, well. You know Miles Davis was asked one night by a female admirer if he performed cunnilingus as well as he performed with a trumpet …'

'Did he fuck her, Ro?'

'I don't know, but apparently he took her to the dressing room and gave her head and she left his dressing fully satisfied.'

'What the fuck's that got to do with anything?'

'I suppose what I'm saying here is that advanced sexual practice is wasted on you pair of white towelling socks, isn't it? Hahahaha.'

Ro gets up throws his bag over his shoulder and eyes the entrance.

'Later, Gents. Oh! Money please, Cheese!'

Martin is trying to calm his cousin Dolly as he thinks he's a bit nervous. Zana is laid on her side and Martin has her right leg over his right thigh. He aims his dick in to penetrate but Dolly is shaking and it's putting both him and Zana off. She's trying to get Dolly hard but it's not working.

'You wanna wait, Dol?'

'No, no. I'm OK. (He re-evaluates) Oh fuck it, OK. Yea, I'll wait.'

Martin and Zana start fucking as Dolly looks on and tries to remember all the things he thought he would be feeling when he finally got to do this but the fantasy's edge doesn't materialise. The house stinks, the carpet stinks, the sofa stinks and most who are in attendance look way past their best years, with Zana being the exception.

'Have some sniff, Dol.'

Martin pulls out his wallet from under the pile of thrown clothes as his arm is going back and forth in time with the motions of sex and Dolly struggles to get it out of his hand, which makes the scenario even more awkward. Dolly lines three up on a random CD cover he finds near the armchair they are all laid next to. He throws it up his nose and places the CD case on the arm of the chair.

Martin and Zana are in full swing and Dolly starts to become engrossed. Martin leaves most standing in the filth department. His appetite for hard sex and deviancy is the stuff of legend on the Strip. Martin is one of the longest serving representatives and his standing with the Money Pattern can offer up to more than ten potential sexual opportunities a month.

'I'm coming.'

Zana presses against him and fixes herself still as he bangs, bangs, and bangs.

'You can come in me, it's alright, just fucking …'

'OH, FOR FUCK'S SAKE!'

Martin pulls it out, he didn't hear her and he produces a fair amount of semen that rises well over the top of his clenched hand. Zana laughs and turns to Dolly who then offers his penis for her to suck. She does this immediately and after what was turning out to be a pretty bad experience for Dolly, the mood changes and he finally starts to see what the fuss is all about. The drugs helped obviously, and much to everyone's surprise he manages to start forming an erection. Martin watches for a while before reaching over to the CD case and his drugs. He readies four lines and takes two.

'Two on there for ya, Zee. Don't let greedy guts have it all.'

Zana has Dolly's penis up to its correct form. Dolly looks at the CD cover:

'I had some already, mate.'

'I know you did, you goppy twat!'

Zana pulls up and reaches for the CD cover.

'Mart, get me a drink.'

'Yea, me too, mate. Ta.'

Martin pulls his jeans and boxers back on and walks into the kitchen. In various rooms there are groups of people having sex, a couple are on the stairs, various pools of people are scattered around talking and in the kitchen he's met with three people in mid conversation:

'Hi there. Sorry, can I just grab three beers?'

One of the three is Rohit who turns to make space and recognises Martin as he reaches over to take the cans.

'You Tunnel's mate? You work at the Bullet, don't you?'

'Yes, mate, on both counts. How is the flaky bastard?'

'Haha. Tunnel? Haha. Yea, he's alright. I just left him actually.'

'Is he still at the shop?'

'Yea, he's manager now, mate. I'm Ro, by the way.'

'Martin.'

'You want some of this?'

Ro offers Martin a spliff.

'Oh lovely. Hold on, you know Cheese, don't ya?'

'Yes mate, just saw him too - at the Hippo actually.'

'You, 'erm, got any of that on ya? Cheese has mentioned you before for weed, like.'

'I have, mate, yes. 25 a pop. It's good Jamaican, subtle, doesn't knock your head off.'

'I'll have some then, as long as it's not that twigs and seeds stuff.'

Dick

The streaming wasn't so great after 56 hours of continuous use. The computer was old and it looked really shit as well. But up until now it had served a decent purpose, that of enabling Coreen to watch as much pornography as possible; and on days where a small measure of normality occurred, namely to check her emails and manage her band pages, the computer also justified its existence. Her new music was in abundance, it was the only thing that got her out of bed to be honest; that and work. But the curtain had finally fallen for want of a better fucking word and Coreen was becoming more and more entrenched in activities that were destroying her. Currently she preferred amateur films done by couples who would place the camera rather messily on the side of wherever and then go about fucking in front of it. She started to like the fatter women and men instead of these fucking hard bodied studs and the like, because it was all too much like fake bollocks after a while. Literally. There was something about the way non-actors fucked each other that she found more gratifying but the computer wasn't having it, it was making whirring noises and the films were stop/starting. I mean it could have been something else entirely, but Coreen was convinced the streaming was fucked because the computer was also fucked.

She didn't fancy dressing up anymore either; she just wasn't feeling it tonight. She sat in the office chair in her parents' spare room in a short dress she'd bought a while ago - no top on or bra - only stockings, heels and a pair of knickers. Coreen liked to soak her knickers in the warm water because they kept their desired shape better when wet. She arranged them carefully pulling the sides of them upwards tight, so tight that between her buttocks a rash was now beginning to settle itself in for the evening. Coreen liked that *Baywatch* '80s look regarding her underwear, high sides giving her minimal cover around her vaginal area. It looked sexy, and when she dabbed at the whizz it generally sent her to Pluto as she paraded around the house looking in the various mirrors. There had also been an addition to these bouts of solitary porn and drug binging which came in the form of a giant strap-on she'd bought recently. She'd position it so it crept out of the side of the mirror's view to look like she was actually going down on someone. It was thrilling to start with it, looked great she thought, but after a while even that felt basic. As much as it was OK to take regular dabs on the little bit of speed she had left it was becoming more and more obvious that after nearly 58 hours sat around the house doing this, the drug intake had to be raised, the quantity consumed had to be greater.

It felt like an athletic sprint that she was watching, like she was a spectator in close proximity at a hundred yard dash. The slice of sharp air you get when someone passes you at a pace. But in this case they were coming from all directions, almost surrounding her as she sat slumped in the office chair. It felt like they were trying to tell her it was time to stop, that she had done enough of this for now. She imagined that they were making their presence more felt because they cared for her and they were telling her to start being kind to herself again, to rest and recover, and she loved them for it. She knew they were good people, she wasn't afraid of them because right from the start of this, when she had moved back to her parents' house, they were there and it was like she knew them straight away from first contact. Sometimes she sensed them very frequently and at other times, nothing, for long periods.

The Gun Room was above the garage and it boasted a good range of period weapons with a couple of used modern revolvers thrown in. Pete liked his guns and most were collected over a small period of time when the family could finally afford to move into a bigger house. Coreen had issues with this, not because of the guns directly, but because well, she thought it was fucking cheesy. Her dad loved the whole cowboy thing, the barn dances and leather waistcoats and her mum Pattie went along with it, you know, fucking learning all these daft cowboy dances and everything. Anyway, this passion for all things Hi Ho Western was on fine show in the Gun Room. It was her dad's little retreat. The Hungerford Massacre changed everything though and Pete had to get every single weapon 'pinned,' to comply with the new laws. He hated doing it, to him the weapons had now lost their balls:

'They're fucking useless, duck. Fucking useless now. I may as well of bought a load of fucking toy ones in town.'

After Neal woke the house up one night screaming, it was the start of an entirely new phase in the Gun Room's role however. Coreen's brother was far more highly-strung than herself. His behaviour at home currently was a rollercoaster ride on most occasions, incoherent, messy; so when he declared that his TV was floating about 10cm above his bedside cabinet, leading him to scream his fucking face off, the rest of the family listened but took it with a pinch of salt. It wasn't until Pattie woke one night to find an old man counting what looked like 'tall piles of fucking pound coins with his bleedy intestines hanging out' from the side of the wardrobe that the family started to take the idea of the house being haunted more seriously.

Pattie knew a woman called Tina, who she visited from time to time to have her palms read. Tina was a twat really and Coreen didn't like her because she thought Tina was taking her mum for a fucking ride. 75 quid for 30 minutes palm reading was a fucking rip off in Coreen's eyes and when she turned up one afternoon with mum and immediately headed for the Gun Room, Coreen became incensed.

'What was Tina doing here, Mum?'

'She came to look at ya dad's room. We think these happenings are related to the guns.'

'Oh, for fuck's sake. Is she a spiritualist now then? Come on, Mum!'

'Tina knows what she is doing Coreen and don't be so cheeky, she's helped me!'

'She's fucking helped ya spend money, Mum. I'll give her that.'

'She tried to help you remember.'

'Well it didn't help me. Alarm bells rang after the first session.'

'Why did they? What happened then?'

'I haven't told you because it upset me.'

'Well, you were alright in the bloody car on the way home if I remember rightly!'

'Well yea, I was because I didn't want to upset you! But she did a funny thing to me, I can't quite explain it really but it felt like a trick of the fucking trade to be honest. Some bullshit bog standard procedure to rip me off, a kind of basic hypnotism anybody could learn. It didn't feel right. The bullshit nature of it really pissed me off. She's a fucking fraud, Mum!'

'What did she say?'

'She said that in a previous life you were *my* daughter and I was a struggling single parent selling, and you are not going to believe this, DRUGS! To get by, because apparently we were skint. She said that one day you had found my stash whilst I was busy doing something. You then allegedly consumed them all and then died from a fucking overdose. I mean come on, Mum! It's like she's been watching too much fucking TV.'

'I like Tina, she's in touch with all that business. I'm sorry you feel that way about her. She could've helped you.'

'Oh fuck off, Mum!'

Pattie and eventually Pete came to the conclusion that Tina was right about the Gun Room. Tina explained to them that the some of the older guns had bad histories. Histories of violence through being weapons of war and, as such, were now the hosts to these restless spirits, these historical victims that were connected to them, 'bound together through the marriage of murder, Peter!' The spirits needed to find peace and Tina suggested she spend the afternoon performing 'a cleansing ceremony to finally give peace to these tormented souls.' At one point Tina also claimed that Pete's antique Springfield Model 1861 was responsible for scores of Confederate deaths, because she had seen a few of the infantry men on the landing near the bathroom. 'They wore light blue, didn't they, Pete?' Tina connected this with said rifle because it was a popular weapon of choice with both the Confederates and the Union Armies during the American Civil War. Pete fell into a pit of utter astonishment at this news and it made Coreen hate Tina all the more. It was 'fucking bullshit,' she thought.

'Just think, Coreen, there's ten or so Confederate soldiers watching you eat that fucking pork chop. How crazy is that!'

Whatever it was flying around Coreen in the office on this early Sunday evening didn't matter to her. She wasn't interested in the character description, she just knew that whoever it was in the room with her at this moment understood her and looked beyond the activities at hand; the zesty porn, the dressing up, the speed. They were telling her in a fashion that this phase of her life was nearing a conclusion, that it must now change for her. She lurched slightly, back and forth, whilst trying to masturbate. She reached for more drugs and tried to make more room in the confines of this small area. After a while the phone went as she gulped a small measure of cold tea from a cup she made hours back, but she ignored the call obviously. The number wasn't recognized plus the computer had started to work again. Then a text came through.

'Hello mate its Pamla ya alright?

'Can you drive Zoe to Dicks house to pick up some more do-dar?

'She said she'll pay ya mate with a bit of it. I wouldnt normally ask mate but We've near enough run out here and Col is starting to worry about it and you're the only one we know who's got a car. Lol!'

'Oh fuck that,' Coreen thought. It was Sunday, 7.42 in the evening and she'd been up since Friday morning. She had work on the Friday until 2pm then she hit the Millers at four for a pint and it didn't stop from there. However she hadn't touched a drink for nearly 12 hours, if her maths were correct, so driving wasn't completely out of the window. But who was Dick? Coreen looked at what was now another frozen screen on her computer. The bloke's cock was just about to go into his wife's mouth. She texted Pam.

'Alright Pam ya alright? Yea I'm OK mate thanks. What time you want me there? Who's Dick?'

'Oh thanks Coreen we really appreciate this. Dicks from town he's the one who we see for it. Zoe is here now.'

'OK, I'll be there in 20 minutes.'

Coreen took her costume off and threw it wherever. Nobody was coming home for another week. Neal was away with Mum and Dad on holiday, *the sad twat. Who goes away with ya fucking parents on holiday?* She threw her joggers on, a long T-shirt, trainers, and left the house.

At the side of the road across from Pam and Col's flat, holding her one year old daughter Millie, stood Zoe. Coreen parked in the customer area near Next and Pet Stop as it was easier to turn around. She signalled to Zoe and she crossed an otherwise dead high street.

'Alright, bird. How are ya?'

Zoe peered into the car, with baby loosely resting on her left arm.

'Aye up, bird. Can't they look after Millie?'

'Fuck that, mate. I wouldn't leave me coat at their fucking house, know what I mean. Can we stop off at Mallan Close? My new bloke has got the baby seat there for her.'

Millie stared at Coreen through the rear view mirror as Zoe hurled them both in through the back left hand passenger door. Zoe fumbled with the seat belt and tried to wrap it around both her and Millie, eventually giving up. Coreen didn't see the copper coming in from the right, it was as if the he had appeared like a police genie, rubbed into service by some Neighbourhood Watch twat sweating behind a net curtain with a phone pressed against their fucking ear.

'Hello there.'

The officer knocked on Coreen's window. She was, however, so dulled from the speed binge that even the biggest surprise would outwardly look as if it hadn't startled the subject in question. She rolled her window down and the policeman shook his head at Zoe.

'You can't drive with a child in the car without a child's seat.'

Zoe barked at him:

'That's where we are going now! To get the seat!'

'Well that's fine, madam, but as I say it's against the law so you are going to have to find other means of travel.'

'What fucking walk!? With a one year old baby!'

'Please don't swear, madam. It's against the law, should you have a bump up the road then it could be extremely dangerous for your child.'

'Yea, I know that and that's why I'm gunna be careful, officer. I've no other means of getting up to where I need to go, so please can you just allow me to do this, thanks.'

The officer paused, looked at the car's interior, and allowed them to carry on. Zoe was well known to the police. Coreen knew this too. She knew the copper suspected they were up to no good but she didn't care. She wasn't over the limit and they were driving out of town anyway. The chances of them being followed were fucking slim, the law didn't care that much, far too much hassle. They were followed for just a short while as they drove to Zoe's bloke's and then the copper disappeared.

Zoe's new boyfriend leapt out of the front door clutching the baby seat, like an untrained dog. His face was covered in spots from all the fucking clucking, Coreen guessed. He looked depressing. Coreen sank.

'Alright? E are …'

'Tar.'

Much to Coreen's surprise Zoe fitted the car seat in herself while her new bloke held Millie. It was nice to see Millie in the seat and safe, Coreen thought. She was a beautiful little girl and she seemed to like the hard rap that was coming out of the system.

'She likes that, mate. Haha.'

Zoe's bloke waved them off. 40 minutes later they were in a McDonald's car park after going through the drive-through. Dick was now in the car along with a mate of his, a large chuntering kid called Balloon.

'I fucking needed something, mate. I tell ya, been up for fucking weeks, hahaha.'

Dick spat most of his fries over Coreen. He was sat in the front seat because he needed to give her directions before they stopped for food. His drugs were hidden all over the Key Hill area of town due to the coppers raiding his flat a day earlier.

'I know you from somewhere. You used to go to Raincoat, didn't you? Back in the day …'

Coreen was trying to fight off her almost immediate repulsion for Dick. He was about her age, ravaged by whatever drugs he routinely took and he also looked incredibly violent; the kind of violent streak that can't go back. It all started to get very, very dark. Coreen hid within herself.

'Yea, I did, Dick. Good club.'

'Was fucking brilliant, want it.'

Dick turned to Balloon who was sat directly behind him. Zoe was in the middle and Millie beside her:

'Ya gunna have to get Malc Mitchell to get that other thing cos I ain't driving round there tonight.'

'Yea, no prob.'

'Zoe, I can't give ya yer normal thing cos I ain't got it. It's gunna have be to half of that.'

'Oh fucking hell, Dick …'

Dick flew into a micro rage:

'LOOK, THE FUCKING COPPERS HAVE BEEN ROUND. YOU'VE JUST SEEN WHERE I PICKED MY FUCKING MAIN THING UP FROM, ANT YA? I AIN'T GOT THE SPACE TO GET MORE IN AT THE MINUTE, DUCK.'

'Alright, well look, I'll come back next week if it means getting the same amount off ya.'

Dick had calmed down. He lit a fag. Coreen thought about Millie.

'Open the window, please.'

'Sorry … yea, do that, actually that might be alright. Things might of calmed down by then. THEY FUCKING RAIDED US LAST NIGHT BUT DINT GET OAT. BUT I AIN'T GOING BACK TO FUCKING PRISON, ZO. FUCK THAT.'

Dick checked the plastic bag he had behind his legs and flew into another rage.

'OH! FOR FUCK'S SAKE. FUCK'S SAKKKKKKKKKE!!! WE NEED TO GO BACK, CAN YA GO BACK PLEASE, MATE!!!'

Coreen finished her milkshake.

'What's up?!'

'I'VE FUCKING DROPPED TWO GRANDS WORTH OF FUCKING CRACK NEAR OUR NANA'S! FOR FUCK'S SAKE!!! CAN WE DRIVE BACK, PLEASE?'

Coreen tried to calm him down slightly and kept looking at Zoe, who had a look of 'we have to do this, Coreen' written all over her face, through the rear view mirror. Balloon was also trying to calm Dick down. Coreen fucking hated this twat and she'd only known him two minutes. She started the car up and asked Dick for a fag, wound her window down and drove off towards the previous destination.

'OH FUCK ME! THERE IT IS! HAHAHAHHAHA.'

Dick had spotted the flattened blue bag of crack in the middle of the road on the way up to his Nana's place. It was a small miracle that it was still there. His bouts of micro rage had now completely taken over his tone of speech.

'I MUST OF FUCKING DROPPED IT GETTING INTO YOUR FUCKING CAR. FUCK ME! HAHAHAHAHAHA! THAT WAS FUCKING CLOSE. COULD HAVE BEEN PROPER HASSLE THAT FUCKER.'

Coreen was past the point of worrying if the law had their eyes on them by now. I mean they were going up and down the same road periodically for what must have been the last hour or so.

Dick reassessed his bag of drugs.

'RIGHT, I'LL GET YOUR THING SORTED, BUT CAN YOU JUST DRIVE AROUND A BIT MORE? GO OVER TO THE FOUR LEAVES NEAR THE VOLKSWAGEN GARAGE. I LIVE NEAR THERE. IS THAT OK, MATE?'

Coreen nodded and headed for the flyover. Balloon had taken a liking to Zoe and they were both laughing in the back.

'BALLOON'S GUNNA BE HELPING ME A BIT MORE, ZO, SO YOU'LL PROBABLY BE HEARING FROM HIM A LOT NOW.'

Balloon had started to fondle Zoe's breasts whilst making some cheap porn noises, Zoe giggled and noticing what was going on, Dick joined in, reaching over and grabbing at her thighs.

'NEXT TIME YOU COME OVER, ZO, WE'LL GET SOME OF THIS CRACK ON THE GO AND FUCK EACH OTHER ROUND MY NEW FLAT AYE. HAHAHA.'

The three of them grabbed at each other. Zoe now had her hands round Balloon's penis and Dick continued making these noises that were part shit porn and part '30s Hollywood monster flick, whilst Coreen tried all she could to ignore what was happening. She eyed Millie, thankfully she was asleep, as they cruised through town. The car was now a sodden sponge that had soaked up too much terror. Coreen folded into the pages of deflation.

'Where do you live, Dick?'

'ACROSS THERE, OPPOSITE THE PUB, MATE.'

Coreen pulled up.

'YOU WANNA COME IN, ZO? HAHA.'

'Shall we Coreen? Half hour?'

'No, we need to go. Pam wants this stuff.'

'PLEASE YASELF THEN. NICE TO HAVE MET YA, MATE.'

'You too.'

Balloon kissed Zoe and Dick put the drugs on her crotch area, pressing them down hard and releasing another Igor-esque porn bark. They both eventually got out the car.

'CALL ME OR BALLOON THEN, IF YOU WANT THAT OTHER BIT NEXT WEEK.'

Coreen looked at Dick, he nodded. She started the car up.

The journey back was silent mostly. Coreen felt like she had done the right thing. They would've fucked each other senseless in his flat and God knows what else. Millie abandoned in the fucking kitchen or wherever. It was too bleak, too depressing for contemplation.

'Fucking cunts.'

Coreen dropped Zoe at her house and bought Millie in for her.

'You couldn't pop up the pub and get me some electricity, could you?'

Coreen eyed the chunk of speed Zoe had given her.

'No, I can't. See ya soon.'

The Ghoul

I think the reality of it was this. The Angel of the North wasn't so much a mirage or a supposed symbol of Northern pride that actually liaised more with the idea of gentrification. Or a posh gesture by some artist with no attachment to what the North had become under successive neoliberal governments. No, the truth was this; that it was an idea that he didn't think of himself and that further added to the state of his mess, his self under this lie he had created. What he really thought about it all happened in this conversation he had with himself after six pints and two bags:

'*The Angel of the North* stands brazen and rust-infested. It makes no call to escapism, yet through its structure the creator understands that all around it yearn for a life. It's simple and effective, perhaps. Any notions attached to it of corruption or backhanders or elitist visions, realised as some kind of political wallpaper pasted over the sociological cracks in the North could go into the night, most probably, between concerned voices around a table.'

He had sat over his laptop writing a completely forgettable book on the gentrification of the North in relation to modern public art in its towns and cities for nearly a year, and he had failed to convince people, once again, that he was credible. On its release the book had fallen to the floor like a crap rocket, it was bloodless and nobody cared. He turned to face another day in which he had achieved nothing. It wasn't even a bonafide failure and he knew it. To be bonafide it had to be interesting, honest even, *original*, but with flaws. It and he were not any of these things in this chosen line of work, the art world, the creative world; these things were like the giant shadow of the Pyramids to his pathetic package tourist, high on Hollywood notions, stumbling around the Valley of the Kings with his shit camera and crap shorts.

The Ghoul looked out over the park from his study; the trees and grass and the path. He drank. He then did something very peculiar. The Ghoul's behaviour went into a set of behavioural patterns that, from the onlooker's point of view, would perhaps conjure up immediate concerns that the subject at hand was suffering from some form of mental illness. Indeed, the Ghoul was, but what he had been doing for a very long time here was enacting other people's behavioural symptoms when suffering from their own psychological turmoil. These were people he knew, successful people in his field who were very prolific with high levels of renowned creativity who, at various points, had disclosed to him in great detail how they would personally suffer on a regular basis with depression, and what it would make them do to try and escape it. The Ghoul believed this to be a kind of creative turmoil that would greatly enhance their work and arriving at this realisation, the Ghoul decided he would imitate these things in the hope that it would dress his own work:

'I mean it has to, obviously, doesn't it? Look at them! They feed from these voids of despair, it feeds their fucking work!'

His current obsession was checking into cheap hotels and visiting porn sites or dogging forums whilst drinking and taking cocaine. That was his favourite. He marvelled at how this could be. He would take the drug and then immediately browse online. He became fixated with the practice after getting to know a successful acquaintance who did just this. The Ghoul believed himself to be like this too, he would dress his psyche with such approaches and as the night wore on his mound would shudder and his heart would work hard to fight against the power of the cocaine wrecking his unfit meat. It was hard work but the Ghoul persisted. It was all very depressing to enact, but he was convinced it would aid his substandard art. He would play it right down to the finest detail in the information disclosed to him by his latest source.

What is it in the reflections that bend up and down and sideways as the Ghoul glanced 360 around the pub? It was a slow broken 360, gathering data that went out as fast as it came in. The old ceilings and trims that hung under the lips of the century old roofs and the houses they belonged to scattered the view as drink was had and silence dominated. The frown became deep and matched the width of the Ghoul's Marlboro as he threw it down his fucking mouth outside the pub. Email to 'X,' email to 'Y,' text to 'Z' and a tweet that when read didn't really work and made him look like a cunt. It was shit, it was all shit and shit wouldn't go away because even when it wasn't shit it was shit.

The throat will only hold out for a time and then it's too late, too late for you. It will scream for help but that will be too late too.

Cancer will have it, it will have you after a time and what did you do when it sought battle with you? You did nothing. You had an affair, you wanted to feel titties and rub yourself against whomever. To feel alive in this city trap, to hold course through its streets and impossible networks of communication and chance meetings, to win, was shit business if you were useless and the Ghoul was a grey entity; a short depressed man full of bones that hid under exhausted nicotine-ridden muscle. Life was a piece of fucking fly shit and he was a chicken, a directionless farm chicken with vague mental flashes of purpose that his body would jolt to; a trail of seeds, a drink of whatever, the route to sleep. The farm.

The exhibition was held at the Temp Gallery in the Martin District about a mile from the small city centre. The building hired for the event was an Edwardian structure, an old school that now housed various small businesses and on occasion art shows from local people or visiting artists from the bigger cities. The Ghoul had one faintly strong hand that could be passed for reputation, in the form of a series of body designs for Dyson handheld hoovers at the start of the noughties, that sometimes got him the opportunity to put on 'shows' at smaller exhibition centres. Tonight the Temp Gallery was such a place for him and he had travelled up specially on the train. His theme was black rubber Kit Kat wrappers (to size) with small bits of roughly cut mirrored glass attached to them, and the small exhibition itself was entitled 'Consumption.' It was shit, of course.

This was typical of him, of the Non-Creative, trying to combine elements that didn't work. Entities that were completely alien from each other wasn't the issue, it was in the selection, the understanding where ideas grew, not in the unaesthetic; you just simply don't go to the Shock Shop for an easy purchase. It was almost as if he'd decided to watch Michael Mann's 'Manhunter' whist taking ecstasy.

22 people turned up to the exhibition and they were the kind of people that were hated by every single person ever, the type of people that were even hated by fucking ghosts who had had no connection whatsoever to them in any previous life. Even passing cats and dogs would bark and hiss at them aggressively as they smoked outside intermittently. Passing babies in prams would throw half-eaten biscuits at them and shit their nappies in protest at such heinous fucking people. The Ghoul paced the corridors waiting for feedback, politely giving way to anyone walking in the opposite direction along these slim passages dressed in thick gloss paint that had seen two world wars and thousands upon thousands of people.

What a pitiful waste of anything this evening was as people said goodbye with parting comments that he didn't believe, but there was some solace here this evening in the form of a hotel on top of the hill which led up from the Temp Gallery. The Ghoul had once again orchestrated an opportunity to enact his version of the tortured artist. He mumbled some directions to the exhibition's director about where to send the pieces on show off to. The director smiled and enthusiastically followed the instructions not flinching once at the Ghoul's arty stupidity but instead engaging wholeheartedly to the point where you almost wondered if the exhibition did, after all, carry some notable merit. But no, it didn't. That much was true as he stepped out onto the slim street, which travelled steep on its way to the hotel, a street that ignored him. The Ghoul was a fat copyist cunt.

The Ghoul wanked as hard as he could over 'Suki,' the forty-two-year-old housewife peeking out of his laptop. He pulled aggressively at what was a grey and pungent semi-hard penis that looked like it had a bad wig on. He arranged his trouser tops just underneath his bollock sack so as not to reveal too much flesh and withered leg. Suki was expensive, 50 pounds for ten minutes and she had a timer on her camera. The Ghoul became annoyed at her occasionally looking at it whist bellowing sex noises as she frigged herself on her shit pink bed, but he didn't let on. He was fucking off his head but also conscious he looked coked up and didn't want to, as it looked bad, but as swaths of the drug came over him he fell in and out of all concern and grunted at Suki like he had all the power; the keys to her destiny were his. What a cunt. She said goodbye and went offline. The Ghoul browsed over more sites and profiles and did two thin lines on the tabletop before fixing another lager. The window to his room opened sufficiently enough for him to throw a cigarette down his throat and to his left, as he perched out of the window, was a semi constructed stage in the middle of the outside area of the hotel. The hotel was over 200 years old and very expensive, but he couldn't be bothered to enact his adopted fantasy out in another Travelodge, he hated them. They were dirty. He flipped his credit card for the Bay Hotel, which overlooked the most prestigious living area of the city he was visiting. The small chrome stage with its shit disco lights at each side looked totally stupid in its beautiful Georgian surroundings. 'It could have been fucking better than that,' he thought. 'Just looks fuckin cheesy.' Milli Vanilli's 'Girl You Know It's True' fell out of the bar from below as somebody opened one of the giant glazed doors that led to the smoking area positioned just past the makeshift stage.

Gallows Hill

The leaves would speak to you via branches. They channelled voices, multiple voices that on leaving the tree's mass would then use the wind to communicate. In very small doses, just enough for anyone who wanted to hear it. I mean really hear it. It was here for anyone that wanted to feel it around them; the sounds were such that they creaked in the silence, sounds that were nothing, sounds that belonged to it all - here on the mound.

The Tower lurched over the hill and kept watch on its stone and gate with the help of slanted wood that hung from holes in the highest point of its structure. These were the Tower's eyes and they were all-seeing, channeling a discipline through its pimps who in turn would inject the workers with hard crack or make them chase until they cried for help from the blue and white-collared power walkers in bright trainers pounding the route to work in the morning push. But nothing would help them run from the Tower's hold and the fury of the pimps. Not even the drug and alcohol counsellors who made them tea in the safe refuge on Mansfield Road. Nothing could save them. The arms of the pimps would act fast dragging the workers back into it; the pimps obeyed the Tower in return for supernatural nourishment that would permeate their rule over the workers. This was the process and there would be nothing you could do and you would be stripped and shagged and burnt inside, hollowed out and destroyed. Some of the workers would talk to their fresh vomit behind the houses that were empty. They believed the discoloured fluids they retched up to be on their side and they would confide in the puke because it was part of them. They would damn the Tower and the pimps before the pools of vomit and spit into them with screams and clumsy dance.

Blue plastic sheeting and large abandoned bricks lay all over and the houses that were occupied along the boulevard sometimes gave the workers some brief solace as they walked by and saw Edison bulbs against long curtains and in the driveways cars would be stationed too. Surrounding the workers and for as far as the eye could see were clipped trees that looked like part of a nice European suburb. If you looked hard enough the wheelie bins that were scattered around the trees could be passed off as giant green tree shoes and if you had had enough in your veins then the trees would look at you and fill you with horror because they obeyed the Tower too. The trees would look at you. They would stare and tell you that you were to be fucked, people were going to fucking shag you.

The thick black Victorian railings surrounded the tombs and shattered stone and gave the land its fangs. In certain areas the railings looked to have been smashed open by numerous heavy vehicles that may have driven too close to the short path that separated road from fence. The long road was busy all day everyday. However, these bent and gaping holes were no victims to the occasional traffic accident, no. This was the work of the Tower who would, before the eyes of the worker and the pimp, rip the iron in front of them in an occasional display of dominance and they would know that this was terror and nothing before or after this could or would ever conquer it. The worker worked the small path in-between the road and fangs, it was the area for the worker to sell themselves to the cars and the Tower had no time for foolishness and fear from the worker. 'Being sold' was paramount and it pleasured the pimps as they gave out rocks from armchairs in stuffed bags that lay on phones to power the workers and create purpose in the pimp to fucking justify it all. The cars outside grated against the road causing jagged shards of metal to fall onto the ground as they moved like slugs, eyeing the beaten workers over dashboards, wanting them in an almost carousel motion.

At the center of the tomb yard was a giant hole and at the bottom of the hole there stood a withered blossom tree that watched all things around it with eyes given to it by the Tower. The hole was full of graves, some headstones were horizontal, in a stepping stone fashion and they trailed off in no particular direction. Behind and all around were its walls that were littered with vaults, a mausoleum housing more of the dead from the Great War. The gate that led the daytime observer into this was locked so you had no choice but to marvel at the sight behind the high railings that stood on top of the small walls along its winding path en route to the bottom. The tomb yard as a whole wasn't easy to navigate and translate visually and its energy, its power, was something else entirely. The men who fucked each other here, who came on foot late at night would favour the sloping hill behind the tomb yard, which fell onto a wide tarmac walkway. It's here that a figure called The Dog would appear - a man feared even by the pimps. The Dog would orchestrate hard orgies in the furthest pits of the wall that separated the tomb yard from the sloping hill under the trees that yanked their roots up from the ground to sprawl out like a dead octopus being sold on a market stall, over the soil of this, the Gallows Hill.

The Tower and the Dog were in unison. The Dog would skip and scramble between trees like a cartoon character sniggering and panting, growling. The Tower would protect and power the Dog and gift him with the ability to control the men who came here for sex in ways unimaginable. The Dog would raise and suspend some of the men in mid air for instance and make them watch the sex, he would tease them as they waited for their turn whilst he stalked the outer perimeters looking for more ways to get his cock sucked. He would arrange his trousers so that the waist of them was just above his knees and he would hold this position tight with his belt revealing the tops of stockings. This powered the Dog so madly he gasped with a slow murmur of complete and utter abandon as he commanded all to look at him. The iron benches that sit along the wide walkway were cold and dirty and surrounded by mud. No grass grew here just the odd plastic bag that would get caught in the benches legs as the Dog walked and fucked men hard with all the might of the Tower's beam that came from its eyes at the highest point from the slanted wood driving itself into the Dog, the light from the moon behind the Tower and the street lamps below and all around it would set a scene that even daylight found hard to smother. It was a stinking hole, a land filled curse that ruled over the side of the hill and dominated the area more so than the old lace and ale factories. It held a miserable permanent power that infiltrated those that wanted it.

The central heating hummed then spluttered at its required time sending a mild tremor through the house. Through the window the next-door neighbours were busily activating the push into a new day. Jakub's bed lay across his small room and the curtains were never shut. His bed was partly surrounded by large cans of lager some of which he had used as ashtrays according to what part of the bed he had been sitting on or which corner of the room he had sprung from. He liked to use his room well when he was (in his words) 'On Heat' and in the coil of a session that transformed his life from a nothing experience into the thrill of everything, ever:

'Press ups, sweat and porn. Press ups, sweat and porn.'

His bed would never have a quilt cover on, although he did have several and sometimes at night he could feel things on him. He could feel things moving in his ears and he worried about that as he tried to arrange the quilt so the bit that reeked of sweat wasn't under his nose. 'This was the end,' he often thought. It was always the end.

Underneath Jakub's bed was a large bin bag full of stuff and he could feel its bulk through the thin mattress. There was also a faint smell of cooking oil in the air because he liked to rub it on his tits when he'd pose in front of the mirror so they gleamed, a kind of makeshift baby oil effect that he still wasn't sure about. The bin bag under the bed needed attending to but he couldn't lift a finger. He couldn't even move the squashed lager can that stunk of stale flat beverage, as it stood bent near his face. Behind it in an intertwined mess were three different coloured damp stockings, hold ups in pink, beige and white. They too possessed a mild smell of sweat and dirt. He lay watching next-door open and close the fridge and talk over their shoulder to whomever it was, enjoying the normality of it all whilst rolling a generous dogend from one of the empty cans into a paper, his chest heavy with panic and nicotine and loss, loss of anything. Life slipped away like last week and the willingness to combat this was a part time employee that did the bare minimum and less than that when his back was turned. The creak of floorboards in the room opposite worried him too as he'd stolen all of his flatmate's porn and most of his money in the jar on top of the fridge. The night's cigarette smoke that snuck out through the bottom of Jakub's closed bedroom door was probably hanging on the stairs and that too bothered him. But what was his flatmate going to do? Hit him? No chance. He'd not seen Luke hit anyone in his time. He'd not seen any of that from him and knew violence was a no-go for the man. Luke's door finally swung open and he scuttled down the slim staircase and into the bathroom past the kitchen. The shower barked for five minutes and Jakub lay still as Luke went through his usual rituals that ended with him leaving the house with only a mild slam of the door. Jakub pulled at his cock until he came and finished the fat roll up which judging by the masturbation content must have had some weed in it. Jakub the Dog felt calmed and realised his initial panic attack had been a tad unrealistic. The bedroom didn't smell that bad and outside the grey sky slouched into the afternoon.

Glaisdale Drive

The sausage cobs were the highlight as Ben charted the crap map in his head. When the cob van arrived the misery weakened and the giant torture chamber on Dale Road that housed the heaped mass of used sofas, its walls all emulsion white and flaked, cowered under the imagined light that shone from the Cob Van; like a kind of Industrial Estate *Ark of the Covenant* ripping through the bodies of the opposing army which, on this particular battlefield, were the piles of used fucking sofas. Towering heaps of upholstered lumps that intimidated anyone that feared mind-defacing unskilled labour. The van's sides were brilliant chrome, the top and back were white and hard and thick. The front of the van was like any other in its range; peaky and built to specification for life as a vessel to merge with industry, and in this case the van acted as the grand merchant of wet chicken and offal sold to those who took the whip, who hated the whip and who died by the whip. Ben was skint but he knew the cob van wouldn't let him starve. He knew this because his ex-girlfriend's mum worked in the kitchens that prepared the food. He knew there would be a cob with his name on it.

'Sausage and Bacon, large? Ben.'

'Oi mate, see them two houses over there?'

The big local bloke prodded Ben's arm, snapping him out of the fixed focus he had on the approaching van and pointed to two of the semi-detached flat tops on the street opposite the warehouse.

'Yer, what?'

'I'd stay away from them, mate. I've heard they're fucking roofless hahahahahaha.'

Ben laughed, that was funny, but again he wondered how the big local bloke could be so fancy free in his mind as he sat in his assigned front row seat everyday at the picture house to watch his own being get shredded - fed feet first into a mincer by featureless figures as Westlife's cover of 'Mandy' blasted out of a radio behind them. Ben headed for the van kicking the corners of any sofas blocking his way.

'Tell Karen tar for this will ya, mate? Is she alright?'

'Will do, Ben, no prob mate. Yes, mate, she's sound.'

'How's Nutter?'

'Haha. Nutter reckons *you're* the fuckin nutter, mate! Hahaha.'

'What's she been fuckin sayin?'

'I don't fuckin know, mate, just work talk, I don't fuckin listen really. You two was as bad as each other, want ya?'

Ben's cob felt damp and slightly cold. A sign he thought of the growing distance between his former situation and his emerging existence as a reborn fucking waster, a weird waster at that, one that tortures himself at night with drugs and masturbation over imagined scenarios of his ex getting fucked by random blokes in town. This would be a cardboard box type journey into visual despair powered by the wet and cold cave that had become his mind. His hand-shandy workout was always so intense, so repetitive that by the morning his cock would look like a withered red tulip, but not as big. Like a midget albino triffid between his fucking legs. The meat cob made Ben fart almost instantly on full consumption but this had its advantages. The 12 minute or so intervals between each fart made clock-watching go faster. The stench was welcomed, plus your own odours are often mild pleasurable aromas that transport a moment's satisfaction and this carried Ben through. Even those that were in his immediate vicinity casually shrugged each creeping smell off with a 'dirty cunt' or a 'you fat dirty twat.' It was as if the vulgarity of another's internal waste being released into the atmosphere only faintly nudged these men, these workers. It was a nowhere; a workless existence that was tormented with insane tasks barked out by living gnomes in high-waisted trousers, and it infiltrated these dour vessels and jabbed at their backs causing a slow motion shuffle en route to wherever.

You were worked here regardless of what you were outside. The giant storage spaces laughed at the top of the taxi driver's ear you bit off last Friday. The giant loading spaces laughed at the terror you were capable of outside, a terror you could see running through people's eyes as you rested your hands on the bar and ordered. Some of these lads were hard and they carried hopelessness like a celebrity might carry a chihuahua. Spliffs were smoked on the abandoned floors above the main warehouse as the lads talked about nothing other than what society would allow them to talk about. But Ben wasn't bothered. He preferred the rank coffee and the shift's eight hours in real time, any scrap of internal abandonment via the aid of illegal supplements was always enjoyed more constructively outside of work. The bus would crush him, not literally, but you know, those journeys were the opportunity for paranoia as it morphed into intense depression taunting him as he rode through the estates with all of their memories of when he had a good job and a cognitive standing in life. Where he could cling on to the mindlessness and laugh inside the corrugated sheet metal box his skull was nailed into. He had it all for somebody that had nothing. It was everything he needed in the trap. The trap allowed him to reach out occasionally, do risky things like buy porn mags at the local newsagent where they knew his face, at 6.30 on Sunday morning, but he never quite got anywhere near those blokes in the pornos. No, he wasn't really cut out like that. He just liked the thought of it.

The Gudgeon stood partly burnt out and surrounded by temporary steel fences in the middle of the green across from the small high street. It looked like an old Jacobean barn, black with ash and plastic from a fire that had recently swept through half of it. It contrasted deeply with the rest of life, with contemporary design and the way that the city, a mile away, rose up from the ground and sprawled in interesting and beautiful shapes. These large pockets of human habitation, unremarkable, plain, flat and full of passing curiosity to the outsider were not to be taken lightly. These holes had intricate histories and bore the full weight of oppression, boredom and consistent disorientation. The Gudgeon was so weighted in tragedy that it almost had the same feel as the house on the hill in 'Psycho.' It stood like an abandoned farmhouse, built well before the 20th century and now crumbling in the middle of the green, but at the same time it was still punch solid and full of resistance.

The Gudgeon would not be destroyed because no fucking fire would have it. No fucking arsonist would kill it. It served as the body snatcher to all the young who drank in there. It would be the bridge between youthful vigour and the clamp of addiction. The older drinkers had no time for needles and foil and pipes. They scoffed at wraps. The older drinkers were beaten in other ways; by the black mock Tudor walls and pent up sexual desires that were only realised through drunken danger wanks and minutes lost in late afternoon gazes. They were constantly squashed by misinformation, gathered up and rinsed by mechanical arms, sorted, re-uniformed and put through it again. There was nothing. Nothing.

Ben rolled with the bus through the slim lanes that housed the bus route:

'Hello there. I'm wondering if you buy second hand jewellery.'

'We do, yes.'

'I've got an old engagement ring, cost me 450 pounds, two small diamonds, really small, platinum ri …'

'Look, I can tell you now you won't get 450 for it anywhere, it doesn't work like that, but I'll have a look for you.'

'Yea, I know. I've called round most places, I wasn't going to sell it, but you know.'

'Oh yes, I know.'

'Thanks. You're on Shelly Avenue, right?'

'We are, yes.'

'Thanks.'

'Hello, mate.'

'Ben. Got me dough?'

'Yea, I will have later, mate. Can I pop round?'

'Yes, me owd. Buzz me. What time?'

'Bout seven?'

'Sound.'

The bus shook so badly that the introduction of crash bars was months away, obviously. It flew like a bobsleigh past the post war prefabs and large proto council houses onto the big road that led into town. The ring was hard to look at, not because of the person whose finger it used to hang on, but because it reminded Ben that at one point somebody else was sat next to him in a confined space. They would be there daily, sat next to him. It reminded him of being able to eat and to spend money and to do things he wasn't really into but had gotten used to in a routinely safe manner. Now that was gone he operated like a square wheel and through the incineration of his safety net lay the limitless hole of panic.

'I'll give you 35 quid for it.'

'OK.'

'Ello, mate.'

'You coming round?'

'On me way, mate, bout 45.'

'Sound, me owd. Aye, Pop Master's ere. He (laughing) wants to know what you did to his fucking laptop on Friday night. You dirty cunt, it's full of viruses.'

(In the distance) 'You dirty fucking cunt, Ben!'

'Oh fucking joking. Is it fucked?'

(laughing) 'I dunno! This aint fucking PC World, is it.'

'Oh fuck. Tell him sorry.' (loudly) 'Sorry, mate!'

'See ya in a bit, me owd. 30 yea?'

'Yea, I got it.'

Fence opened the door almost straight away as Ben nodded with the air of a man in full apology mode.

'Ya a cunt, you are.'

'Sorry, mate. I'm fucking broke, bro. I got it though.'

Ben handed Fence the 30 quid and walked into the kitchen to find Pop Master sat in the far corner, he nodded and quickly regained his visual fix on John Solly. Solly was stood near the kitchen window opposite the table Pop Master was at. Solly had his hands in prayer form close to his face and was inhaling/exhaling deeply and at fast intervals. Solly then let out a controlled scream punching the air with his right arm whilst his left stayed at the side of his waist, in a kind of karate position.

'What the fuck are you doing, Sol?'

Sol turned slightly.

'Tai Chi, Ben. I told ya, I learnt it years back.'

Solly's eyes were like dinner plates, as were Pop Master's. This was complete weirdness. Solly looked deadly serious as Fence casually walked by him towards the cupboard over the cooker and pulled out a bottle of white wine, turning back to Ben:

'What you up to now then, mate?'

'Fuck all, mate, I got five quid left. Bus fare to work tomorrow, ain't it.'

'Ya a daft bastard, Ben. All ya cash gone on my gear. Good though, eh?'

'Be reet. Yea, was good gear, mate, but fuck, halves don't last two minutes.'

'Don't buy the cunt then, you daft bastard, or at least wait until you've got money to cover a big bag of the cunt and food and every fucking thing else.'

'Yea.'

'My laptop's fucked, Ben,' Pop Master barked over from the table. 'Fucking all kinds of weird shit on it. You're a dark horse you are, you cunt.'

'Ha ha, just porn, mate. Sorry.'

'Blokes in stockings. Fuck are you on?'

Solly snapped out of his questionable Karate moves:

'He's on Fence's shit gear, Pop.'

Fence lined Ben a large trail of drugs on the table and motioned him to come over. Ben whacked it up and sat on the chair opposite

Pop Master. Solly went up the stairs across from Ben and Fence tended to more lines.

Ben sniffed hard and looked for somebody's cigarettes.

'Your laptop alright then, Pop?'

Jelsons

A single white pole in the outer corner holds the porch up. Its outer shell consists of thin white wooden panelling. Behind this is more brick; the attempt at architectural elegance here ensures that the flimsy decorative panels go the whole way around the top of the porch entrance. The window in the top left hand corner of the front of the house directly above the entrance winks at you like the introductory configuration of the monster from the dog kennel before it's taken out with a flamethrower in John Carpenter's 'The Thing.' Lines of these houses scatter the foot of the hills and they are nicer than ours but that doesn't matter. I don't like it round here anyway. It's out of town and the brick is a different colour too. I like the excrement brown bricks from the 1960s council developments that we've got, not these beige bricks laid out by the snazzy new set that are currently in bed with the council.

The junction edges slightly over the road's drop which opens to reveal the hole in the bowl; the land dishes and in it sit the rows of one-eyed creatures. These small living spaces do pull more towards contemporary structure I suppose and their modern arrogance kind of makes a mockery of the other creatures down the hill that stand nearer town, the creatures I live in with their shit coloured bricks; but, in hindsight, those Jelson homes died very quickly. Far quicker than my old place. The paint peeled very quickly on the poles that held the porches and the Jelson estate became like one of those dashing celebrity hedonists from music, film or sport that the papers championed in their younger days. Days that are soon eaten by the ageing process and if, say, the paper bothers to print a small photo of the now deteriorating has-been they look ravaged; cave dwellers almost, hideous hermits. From the bay of the hairdressers that sat near the drop you could see the horror unfolding but this was more than a week's spectating obviously. It called for a lifetime's viewing to get the real gist and so if you lived around here long enough you saw it curdle as you shifted your shit arse to the chip shop, the hairdressers or the paper shop.

The hairdressers is small, so small. Its banana yellow interior and six chairs all sit so uneasily and look like a child's hasty inexperienced positioning in a doll's house. The unit sits in between the chip shop and newsagents. It opens at 9am depending, and the souls that tread its small area scream inside for anything but this, as they eye the body's veins for use as ropes to scale the walls of this unspeakable entrapment. A way out isn't what the careers advisor offered - simply because very few think about one. When there is no demand there is no supply.

Lincoln stood close to all the women on the rectangular table in Westside Bar. The place was busy and he motioned over to Maria who stood at the other side of the table. His arm brushed past all the women on his side of the table but it was Sarah who picked up on the contact.

'Oops, sorry,' he said.

Sarah didn't look at him directly, 'I don't mind.'

Lincoln kept thinking about that. Why did she say that? She was married and he thought that perhaps marriage, well it goes so stale and sex is this thing that searches out for a life of its own with other people outside of that marriage. That it wasn't cheating; no, it wasn't that at all. It was a need to feel like you had pushed away from the concrete slippers those rings gave you both, the impossible monogamy; it was the silent other life. Going through Jelsons and the shops in the car one day he saw Sarah across the road pushing her son in his tractor. She waved at him, but not *at him* if that makes sense. Lincoln wanted to fuck her. He dreamt of it, going to her house wherever that was, it couldn't be far from the shops. He thought about just going there and knocking on the door after say a few more chance meetings and further confirmation, confirmation that it would be all right to do that because he thought it could possibly get to that. He thought about fucking her in the kitchen on the sink pulling her dress right over her tits, banging the hard fuck out of her.

The five gates were the entrance to a wood that walled itself along the top of the hill and stood over the valley (or 'the hole in the bowl' depending on how you saw it) that played host to the sprawling

Jelson estate. Along with this, and at the centre of it all, stood the Belmont Lookout, a grand arched tower erected centuries ago by the Lord of the *Big House,* that was itself built directly in line with the tower but a mile away down the hill. It was built to enable the Lord's men to keep watch on any enemies creeping through the flat lands who might fancy a pop at storming the house and taking what they pleased because obviously in those days they were even bigger bastards than they are now, although that's down to fucking speculation, isn't it? We might think it's all right behind scheduled episodes of whatever fucking soap opera is on, but you know that eventually they'll come through the window; no bastard is safe and the last war was only 80 odd years ago, wasn't it?

The Belmont Lookout lurched from the ground and played guard to the walled woods that grabbed the top of the hill that stood about 30 yards behind it. Lincoln liked to come up here and take speed, watch porn on his phone, walk the slim passages through the woods avoiding the dog walkers, scanning the area, listening, before exposing himself to the trees, high on the sticky base he bought from the dickheads in town. He fucked Iron Face up here one weekend, named so because her ex plunged a hot iron into her face whilst battered on ketamine and acid. She had the outer shape of it permanently imprinted on her face, forehead and crowning the tip of her nose. It had lessened over time but was still very noticeable. Lincoln tied her to a tree with his belt and fucked her in the pitch black at about three in the morning, which was brilliant, because he can never fuck on whizz, it's fucking impossible, but he did that time and that was down to Iron Face demanding he wear her clothes whist he was doing it. That really got him, his cock went crazy, but putting her slim dress on was a problem, to be honest, in solid night; and he ripped it several times, to the point that when he eventually got it on he resembled an 80s darts player going to a fancy dress party as Raquel Welch in 'One Million Years BC.' Lincoln would lose himself in the woods - there was nothing else that quite matched it. The speed, the porn, the fucking and his cock when he showed it to the trees; nothing else came close to this, it was as if the trees knew him, as if they protected him and allowed him to carry on.

'Hi, Lincoln. What you up to?'

Sarah had come out of the hairdressers for change. She leaned against the newsagent's counter tucking her left foot around her right ankle, pressing her waist into the counter packed with secondhand phones and fireworks (it was June). Lincoln was buying fags.

'Nothing much, mate. Work, usual shit. You live up here then?'

'Course I do, you twat. I wouldn't travel across town to work in this shithole, would I? Ha ha ha. Yea, I live on Ermine Close, just up there.'

Sarah pointed to the main road across from the retail units that followed the hill up to its point.

'What about you?'

'I'm on Princess Drive, mate, do-'

Sarah stopped him mid-sentence.

'Fuck me, it's a shithole down there! Now wonder ya always floating about round here, hahahaha.'

'How do you know I'm always floating about round here? You been spying on me? Haha.'

'It's hard not to notice you, mate. I work at the hairdressers full time now, so I see ya most days. What do you do?'

'I'm at the cleaning place near Phil's garage, mate. It's fucking shit but it's money innit.'

'Want you at that agency?'

'What? In town? Yea, it was fucking shit. Three days ere, two days there, fuck that. I need 39 hours, mate, I can't live on 65 quid a week.'

'That about cover ya whizz habit, then? Haha.'

'Oh come on! I don't do that much. Bloke's gotta have some fun, Sarah, for fuck's sake, wink wink. Haha.'

'I ain't done that stuff for ages, ya can't with kids, it's impossible.'

'Your bloke not into it then? Looks like a cunt, hahaha.'

'Cheeky bastard! He likes a drink but nothing else, drink's shit really innit? I mean it's alright but, you know, gets boring.'

'Well, ya know where I am if you fancy a bump, hahaha.'

'Ya luck's in then cos Vincent's closing at two today, kids are at their nan's until eight. Fancy bunking off then for the afternoon? Could walk up to the tower, it's nice up there when it's sunny.'

Lincoln stopped and went through a whole host of mental notes on drop-of-a-hat excuses for half a day. It was 12.22. He was back at 1pm.

'Serious?'

'Yea fuck it, why not? It's not strong stuff, is it?'

'It's base. Of course it is.'

'Oh fuck.'

'You'll be OK, trust me. Just dab at it, won't drive ya mad. What time's Millar back then?'

'He's in Hastings today on a bike do, won't be back until tomorrow afternoon. LUCKY YOU!!! Hahahaha.'

Lincoln burst into the office back at work and sorted the afternoon off. He was good with work, didn't fuck about, so they were OK with it. He told them he had to drive his mum to the passport office, as she'd lost hers and was going away in three days. They were cool with it and he shifted out towards the staff car park pulling out his phone.

'Alright, mate?'

'Andy, you about, mate?'

'Yea.'

'Wanted to grab one off ya, that OK?'

'Yea.'

'Down in ten.'

'Alright.'

Lincoln walked into Andy's flat after he buzzed him in. Andy was sat on the sofa trying to put clothes on his two year old son Lion.

'Lion, what's that then?' Andy said, pointing to a birdlike figure on the top he was trying to get on him. Lion just looked at him and murmured a two year old's grasp of the English he hardly knew.

'You don't know? It's a fucking seagull innit.'

'No, it's not, mate.'

Lincoln couldn't help butting in, at the same time getting his wallet out:

'It's a fucking eagle, Andy. Look at it properly, for fuck's sake.'

'Is it fuck, you bright bastard! It's a fucking seagull!'

'Mate, what's a seagull doing on a toddler's top along with a cow and fucking sheep and a crocodile? Come on, man. It's a fucking eagle, look at its head, for fuck's sake!'

Andy finished dressing Lion then plonked him down in front of the TV.

'Alright twat, alright, we're not all experts like you. How many?'

'One, tar, mate.'

'One? You giving up? Hahaha.'

'Piss off, I'm taking it easy innit.'

'Got company then? I know what you're like when you nibble this shit on ya tod, haha.'

'Yea, kind of. Put it like this, I'm behaving. What you up to anyway?'

'Fuck all, off to Germany tomorrow fer a few days. Jackie's staying ere mind, if you need any more. Going with Nel and Dick.'

'What for? Who do you know in fucking Germany?'

'National Socialism you cunt, that's what I know in Germany. You seen this?'

Andy goes to his bedroom and Lincoln looks at Lion, watching the TV, neon images race across the screen. He wonders if he's got used to his dad's whizz yet, it stinks. The whole flat smells like plastic farts and fresh base.

'Look at this cunt.'

Andy hands Lincoln a photo. In it, Andy, Nel and Dick are all stood at the centre of the remaining stand at the head of the Nuremberg parade grounds. They are all doing the Nazi salute. The photo is partly spoiled and in black and white which makes it even more disturbing.

'Fuck are you doing there? That's not right, is it?'

'Look, I know it's got a bad reputation mate, but National Socialism is the purest form of fucking politics.'

'Right. Well, from what I know it wasn't very beneficial or fucking pure for a lot of people was it, mate? I mean, come on. Pure? I gotta go, mate.'

'Alright lefty, calm down. You need to remember that the execution of a brilliant idea isn't always going to establish itself wrapped around a blanket of harmony. You also need to think about what this fucking country's done to folk too, you cunt. We are all fucking pigs, mate, some of us get to live until we die rolling around in fucking shit all day, and some of us die violently.'

‘I couldn’t give a fuck about this country, mate, or pigs, and what is a Lefty? What’s that? I’m right handed you poor fucking cunt.’

They both laugh, but it’s like comedy night on the terminal ward.

Lincoln stood on the corner of Rice Road as per Sarah’s instructions. From the distance he eventually saw her walking towards him. She looked beautiful, he thought. Her head occasionally bowed into the top of her chest so as to fend off the wind. Her hands casually nestled in her jacket pockets.

‘Alright?’

‘Alright. Tower, then?’

‘Yea, it’s a nice day innit, and look at this.’

Sarah got a small sack-type pouch out of her jacket pocket.

‘My granddad got given this by a mate whose great grandad looked after the Belmont Tower.’

Sarah pulled out a large brass type key from the pouch as they walked along the old road towards the public footpath.

‘Fuck’s that?’

‘You know that door at the base of the tower, yea? It’s for that. My grandad reckons it’s got a staircase inside which leads all the way to the top innit. Could be a laugh, right? Cosy and no cunt could see us. I don’t want Miller fucking being told I was in the woods with ya, not with your rep! Hahaha.’

'Do people talk about me then? Why?'

'Hahahaha. Calm down, para marra.'

They take a slow walk up the footpath and towards the small car park at the bottom of the hill. They both dab at the whizz and stop to roll fags occasionally. Eventually Sarah puts her arm through Lincoln's.

'This fucking car park is the dogging spot, right?'

'How would I know, mate?'

'Haha, come on. I don't care about that shit, Lincoln. It's perfectly natural to want to do those things. If it's what you want to do, then as long as it's not hurting anybody, why not? It's alright in my books.'

'Oh right, you done it then? Fhaw, hur hur.'

'No, I ain't, but you never know …'

Sarah's breathing gets a little short, like she can't contain a thought and Lincoln senses this.

'You want another fag?'

Pellets

'Hit the fuckin middle.'

Nick held the gun steady but still couldn't shoot the 12" record nailed to the shed. The shed was shit, a quirky uneven structure that barely hid the garages behind it. It looked like a kid's drawing, completely featureless yet full of features. Ruffled felt covered its small roof, attached by large round headed nails rusting in wonky rows along the material's edges that pinned it down to the weak wood for eternity. The corners were a lumpy gathering of excess felt that fell on top of itself very badly. There wasn't much thought put in to the equation of measurement, a rough calculation, a moment's action. The activity didn't call for a passionate application.

'Get a fag outta Planet's packet then.'

Nick nudged Ian for the fourth time. Cigarettes were fair game if the packet was left on the armchair and Ian's nana, nicknamed Planet due to her physical presence, never left them anywhere else. They both sucked on the cigarette so hard it collapsed before its time, the filter looked like a ravaged sodden piece of toffee as they sat and leaned against the rear living room window to the house at the top of the back yard. Across from them both, placed against the wall backing on to next-door stood Rocket's hutch. Ian's nana had bought Ian a rabbit two weeks ago but nobody had fed it after the initial rush of interest and fuss wore off. The household gathered around it and made affectionate noises mixed in with grunts of curiosity but after the crowd had dispersed back into the house it sat motionless, soon to be forgotten (eventually it would stagnate in its own waste as the neglect peaked); the hutch a urine-sodden wooden structure with chicken wire nailed onto the front. Face on it looked like a four year old's attempt at making a television out of crap wood and large gauge animal mesh. The rabbit was now dead and the smell carried but nobody touched it, the thought hadn't evolved mainly because the idea of Rocket was almost automatically lost in people's minds as soon as it hit the back yard. Rocket starved and in the days leading to its death it must have eaten a great deal of its own excrement because when they realized they actually had a rabbit and discovered its corpse its head was welded to the floor of the hutch by a combination of the shit it had been propelled to eat and dead maggots that had drowned in the shit whilst feasting sometime after Rocket's demise. The rabbit's brief life and its view from the Hell-themed hutch consisted of the side of the house with its pale grey brick and a door leading into the kitchen. The pathway from the front gate was short and sloped a little. The front gate was crap, a pathetic attempt at aesthetic, small with rusted hinges and bizarrely it opened outwards onto the public path, again this registered with nobody and you just felt like a cunt every time you left the house and exited the gate with its shit engineering. As nobody noticed Rocket's slow agonising death it was almost as if the animal suffered on a day to day basis in sync alongside the conscious manageable suffering of its masters.

'Fuck off you fucking planet! PLANET!!!!'

Ian didn't like being told off in front of his friends and Nana had caught both Ian and Nick giving each other kamikaze piggybacks on the landing. The aim of the game was that the person giving the piggyback had to try and stab the other person on his or her back, or in the knee or foot with a pair of nail scissors. Ian lashed out at Nick, but Nick knew his fucking onions when it came to this game. The pair of them turned and gasped and stumbled in a ball of borderline fury as Nana pounded up the stairs and screamed at Ian with as much vocal force as her 42 a day habit would allow. Nana didn't react to Ian's response as she turned to walk back downstairs.

Nigel spat at Ian through the large cardboard innard he'd taken from the kitchen roll in the house. They'd both gone into the outhouse at the corner of the back yard and Nigel had locked them both in. He then proceeded to spit at Ian through the funnel until the outhouse started to reek of Nigel's phlegm. Nigel laughed. They both stopped after a time and watched as outside on the lawn, Nigel's brother Colin was fucking his girlfriend in a sleeping bag although initially it looked like they were fighting. They both watched Colin's arse go up and down really fast and this confused them, although neither admitted it. This went on for some time until Nigel started spitting at Ian again through the cardboard innards of the kitchen roll and pissing himself laughing. It bored Ian, the revolving door at the dead end. The options drawer was empty even at this stage in his fucking life and he would occasionally hang from the giant tree in the middle of the green down from his house that fed on bin juice as it fell from the skies onto its leaves. The swings in the park down from the giant tree were knackered. They sprang out from the concrete like spikes and the rocking horse over from the swings was like riding a dirt bike blindfolded. The air seemed to almost resent donating its presence as it knotted itself over the back yards and crap garages with their pits to fix cars, where men filled their roles.

'You spunked up, you cunt?'

Ian hated the wanking compos but not as much as his cousin Lal did. Lal lived up the road from Ian's place, his house was the third one to last near Green Lane which ran the whole way from the big houses at the bottom to the top near the back of the school playing fields. Lal was short with rotten teeth, really rotten. They looked like the wall on his outhouse which had all kinds of paint splattered over its inside wall from where Lal's dad would test colours every time he painted one of the bedrooms or whatever the twat was painting next. It looked like someone had puked all over it; chip shop fat, the lightest shade of beige mixed in with brown and bloodied gut lining. He got lots of stick for those teeth but that was the least of his problems when it came to the wanking compo. The wanking competition took place at Nigel's house after school either

Mondays or Thursdays when no one was in until mid evening. It consisted of however many contestants sat around the house wanking until the first one came and he would be the winner, but he had to prove it by running out of whatever secluded room he was in with fresh semen on toilet roll for all the other contestants to see. Nobody wanked in front of each other, but occasionally Nigel would make Lal wank in front of him because he didn't believe Lal ever wanked. Lal would never come for obvious reasons; the sheer brutality involved had the potential to echo through the memory chambers for life.

'Wank then, cunt.'

'I can't Nige, fuck off.'

Lal was in tears on the lounge sofa as Nigel stood over him screaming:

'Wank, you fucking puky teeth cunt! You are a fucking stroker! YOU FUCKING STROKER, WANK!'

Ian was upstairs looking for money in Nigel's mum's drawers and could hear the trouble Lal was getting but ignored the call to help his cousin. Nigel was a hard bastard, fast, a brutal kid. Ian stayed away from all that, better to be the court jester and win over the nutters in school with affection. After finding a few pound coins in the shiny shell-like case on Nigel's mum's cabinet top Ian spat into his loo roll and barged out onto the landing.

'I've spunked up! I've spunked up!'

He ran down stairs and into the living room. Lal was laid on the sofa still crying trying to masturbate beneath his trousers. Nigel was fiddling with the video player.

'Colin's got this porno, you'll come when you watch that, mate. I'm telling you now.'

'I've spunked, I said.'

Nigel looked round momentarily but his glance was so quick Ian automatically knew Nigel had other things on his mind. He'd got away with it.

'You win then, big boy! Haha. But I still wanna see this cunt wank, so I'm putting on this porno of Col's. The cunt will wank then ahahha.'

'Yea, but I win, mate. Game over.'

'Is it fuck! The game aint over cos I wanna see Lal wank! He never wanks!'

'Yea, but you've never seen me wank, ave you?'

'Yea, but I just know, mate, he he.'

Lal was in tears still, but fighting them and that made the situation in Ian's mind nosedive completely. The rockery around the fire in the living room spread each way from wall to wall and the TV sat on the left hand side, resting on a wooden shelf that fitted into the stone mess. Everything was horrible. Nigel finally got the video working but it wasn't what he thought it would be …

'That's a fucking dog. isn't it? She's sucking a dog off! Hahahhahahahahaha.'

Nigel had stumbled across Colin's party piece 'Animal Farm,' the infamous bestiality vid that was doing the rounds. Lal stood up, fastened his belt and grabbed his coat.

'That is fucking weird, Nige. I'm not wanking to that.'

'Next time then chunky teeth!!! Who wants to watch 'The Exorcist'?'

'Oh, go on then!'

Ian had heard about that film, he got permission to call home and told Planet he was having tea at Nigel's. As he put the phone down, Lal walked out the front door.

'See ya then, mate.'

'Fuck off, Ian.'

Ian watched Lal walk up the road. Lal's face grimaced as he moved slowly up the hill. His shit walk and crap shoes. It took Ian back to that time he played him 'My Generation' by the Who in his bedroom, he left the record playing and went for a piss and as he came back into his bedroom Lal was trying to nod his head in time with the music and he just looked wrong. Ian knew it wasn't going to be good for Lal in whatever he did. Lal was lost, not unhappily lost, just clueless.

Nigel decided to spit in Ian's jacket potato that he'd microwaved for him after the film finished. It was bad enough thinking about the walk home in the dark after that fucking film let alone having to leave his tea because it had gob in it. The walk home lasted for hour-type minutes. It was a short walk but obviously the shock of watching a girl his age stab herself in the vagina with a cross made the brief journey ache with dread. There was no one about, the smell of chip fat and that kind of 'fresh' air that you only got in small towns, total fresh air being reserved for seaside towns and forests. Planet was walking down the path with a giant bin bag when he finally arrived home.

'What you doing, nan?'

'Cleaning up your mess. That rabbit died, poor thing. What did you do to it? Maria next door said she saw you fucking shooting the hutch with that pellet gun. Was ya?'

'No.'

'Your dad called too. You better ring him, he didn't sound happy. There's a Bounty in the cupboard for you as well.'

Van

'Ya not right, are ya?'

'What? Fuck off.'

Tyler shook the ketchup bottle and tipped it upside down to retrieve the last dregs. Lauren stared at him waiting for his next words of wisdom.

'What do you mean I'm not right? Ya such a bastard, ain't ya.'

'Alright, don't get wound up. Just messin, ya mardy bastard.'

'I'm not fuckin mardy either!'

'Oi!'

'Well, Mam! Fucking all day every day!'

'No, I'm not!'

'Yes you are, Ty!'

'Pack it up you two, for God's sake!!!!'

Sandra spat half her food out trying to break up the latest round of petty hostilities between them both. Rob just looked on, he never got involved purely because they weren't his natural kids and he felt it wasn't his place to be authoritarian with them. He did whack Tyler once and afterwards Tyler told him he saw stars. He never told Sandra that, but the day after Tyler told him about the force of the punch ('I saw stars, Rob! Hahaha') Rob cried for a while in the loo.

'He didn't need that, for fuck's sake.'

Rob's own three lads picked on Tyler constantly as it was and now it was the turn of Rob to slap T about; a kid subconsciously sick of this chaos, of parents who simply weren't good enough, parents who scraped by nicking somebody else's homework as they struggled to re-create it into their own words. Who was it that pinned those kinds of badges of responsibility onto you? Parents were people you looked at, ignored and hated until you fucking became one. When that happened, and it always did, well then how were you supposed to do anything other than what you knew through the experiences of your own Mum and Dad? A series of shit dominoes forever falling onto each other; the bloodline never stops creating a firm continual history of behavioural mess. The guidelines in a pamphlet won't help, ten pages with some crap arty depiction of a family unit on the cover with the male's arms around everyone for fuck's sake, laid out on the Health Centre waiting room table as you sit there hating the near dead mess in front of you, some bloke riddled with angina, shuffling over to the nurse who called his name, helped up by his daughter who looks even more desperate than he does. We are cocooned in unavoidable misery mostly. Few think to shift this mindset, to shift it away from the negative. The negative is all encompassing and any flash of positivity is kept firmly close to the individual who experiences this. It is not shared to the group, it is kept in close approximation to the singular vessel it originates from. And even at this stage, even in the micro sense it's taken no further because said vessel isn't entirely sure what to do with such an emotion anyway and so it burns out quickly in the brain as the road works return.

The kitchen strangled everything with its dominant theme of *brown*, brown with mustard wall tiles and white grout and it had a carpet too; one of those new Flotex ones that didn't soak up any accidental spills. It was smooth, almost 'felt'-like, deep red with cornflake shaped black bits in it. It was also shit proof, meaning it kept the shit in it like a stamp collector keeps stamps, you know, firmly stuck down going fucking nowhere. When the guinea pig and cat decided to have a crap fest the Flotex started to smell like a small fucking farm. The black cornflake type shapes hid Macey's droppings perfectly and the cat's too if it shit on the right bit. They got rid of it after a year.

The TV morphed in the background, the early evening soap operas full of identical colours to that of Sandra's Kitchen. It murmured barely audible sounds from its plastic casing that fell limp over the knives and forks as they occasionally smashed on plates. The unspoken word ruled but never directed behaviour, a bit like a subplot that constantly gets rejected. Sandra hated the fucking Kitchen with its workstations, each with its own time slot attaching at various times to the day's stages. 'It's mostly fucking boring, Tyler,' she would say from time to time as her son would sit and talk with her on occasion. 'There's nothing really once you have kids, you have to look after them and that's that, it's boring but you have to do it.' These monologues were nearly always delivered as Sandra gazed out the kitchen window. They were never enlightened, just beaten densely with a diluted form of fucking doom that fed into Tyler like a job interview at a supermarket; held in the manager's office, an office full of mindless piles of paper and stationery, discarded points of sale in neon green, chucked in all corners as she/he rattled off an itinerary that sent machetes into your back.

Tyler waited for his moment then moved in.

'Ya not right, are ya.'

Lauren went.

'FUCK OFF, YOU TWAT.'

Lauren threw her pork chop, half-mangled and drenched in tomato sauce, at Tyler and it bounced off the wall behind his head and landed on Rob's shoulder.

'Er!!!!'

Rob made a small gesture of defiance whilst Sandra jabbed in.

'Stop it, Ty!'

Sandra cleared the plates, Rob turned to Lauren whilst signalling to Tyler to help his mum.

'That room needs finishing and I reckon we're done.'

'Took two minutes, Dad.'

'Well yea, good job really. No cunt else was going to do it were they? Where's that foreign cunt gone, do we know yet?'

'Some fucking where in Lisbon, so I heard. That's where he's from innit.'

'Where's fucking Lisbon? I thought you said he come from Portugal? No good, no fucking good.'

'Well yea, he does, Pop. Lisbon is in Portugal innit. Portugal's a big fucking place, Pop. Plasterer is in Tuesday. Reckons he can do it in a few hours and sez it'll be around 80 quid.'

'No good. You need to get rid of the fucking thing, Loz. It's a dead weight. The Town's fucked, it's dying fast. A commercial property in an area like this, especially on a back street is just no good.'

'I know that, I fucking know that.'

'Do you?'

'Well you fucking suggested I buy it, Dad! You fucking told me it was worth the investment! I didn't know fucking Pedro and his merry thieving fucking hands was gunna do a fucking runner, did I? I didn't tell him to do a fucking runner, did I?'

'No No No No, I know. But you've had it too long, Loz, it keeps going from twat to another. It should of gone.'

'And where was I gunna get rent then? Where was I gunna pay the fucking mortgage on it? What do you think slimey cunto would of done if I told him we were fucking putting it on the market, Dad?'

'It's a mess I know. A mess.'

'No, it's not a mess, Dad, it's a FUCKING mess!'

The street behind Canberra Close looked small, like a display model in a meeting room to attract financial backers, and the cars that lined up along its road were knackered and shit or new and shit. Basic rectangular shaped tin with wheel arches, affordable on finance, generic shoeboxes that kneeled before the unsounds that spread in the little lanes, the little houses and little alleyways. The shit cars played host to short journeys across town because no fucker ever drove anywhere else and if they did it was considered a big deal, a real big deal to head out and away from the limits of comfort, narrow-minded chirping and into larger areas, the city perhaps. Where people were bigger, seemed bigger. Where people were way harder than the little men that drank in town, who lurked in pub toilets waiting to pounce on someone they didn't like.

'You want some eggs, Dad?'

'Yes.'

Dode walked back into the house, scratched his head and thought about nothing. He put the pan on and got the plates out, arranging bread to cover in butter and humming some high-energy club tune that was still ringing in his ears from the previous night. He coughed and sniffed and waited for the eggs as his mum occasionally appeared in the distance folding things and moving things. Dode was still the little boy and his father was still the young man who dressed his son's mind in greaseproof paper and nails, expecting him to cope with the world because, in Dol's mind, the world was as he saw it and he didn't have the capability to accept anything else. Dol didn't say a lot to anybody and his boy Dodey was born into a furnace because of it. His mum Kay was battered into nothing from the word go and lived as a spectator in the dead end.

'E are, Dad.'

Dode paced out with the eggs and buttered bread.

'You shunt be going in town really, should ya. Coppers will just keep hassling you, boy.'

'I ain't fucking bothered. What can they do? They got me, dint they.'

'Coppers don't like pervs.'

'I ain't a fucking perv, Dad. I grabbed her fucking arse pissed out me head, that's not pervy.'

'Ya got salt?'

'Mam!?'

Kay poked her head out Dodey's bedroom.

'What?'

'Oh, don't worry, thought ya was in the kitchen.'

Dodey strolled back into the kitchen and swiped the salt pot.

'You should be supporting me, Dad, not calling me a fucking pervert. It's not like you and Tonny wouldn't have done it when you was pissing it up the wall.'

'Difference being me and Tonny wouldn't have just grabbed some fucker's arse boy, you ask first.'

'Fuck off.'

'And plus, that shit you shove up ya nose. Turns you into a fucking monster, boy. Look at ya fucking teeth.'

'I'm getting em fixed.'

'What with?'

'DHSS are paying for it.'

'Ya working though.'

'Yea, told em I want last time I went down and plus works up n down innit. How they gunna fucking know?'

'You need to get ya head sorted, boy. You need to fucking ignore that cunt you married. Fuck her! Now then, and that's me fucking swearing.'

'Hard, Dad, when you got a fucking kid with her. I can't ignore him.'

'You could've fooled me, boy. When was the last time he come here? Ya mum misses him and that cunt don't talk to ya mum. She don't phone her.'

'She's got no phone, Dad, she tried planting it in my skull last Friday. Her and fucking Haley going at me.'

'Stay out of town, boy. Trouble.'

'I ain't fucking staying in, Dad.'

'Go down the Church then, it's quiet, no arseholes bothering ya. Alright it's full of old men my fucking age, but so what. Ya might learn something, haha.'

'The Church is a shithole, Dad, it's full of blokes wetting themselves and the beer's shit. No women, not worth looking at anyway. Fuck that.'

Dol takes two pound coins of a small pile he has placed next to the garden chair he's sat in.

'Get me a paper will ya.'

'Oat else?'

'Ask ya mam.'

Dode collects his shoes from the back wall outside.

'Mum, ya want oat?'

'Where ya going?'

'Shop.'

'Get some milk, paper for him.'

'Already on the list.'

'How ya doing, mate?'

Tyler pinches the side of Dode's waist as he's checking the dates on the milk.

'How are ya, mate?'

'Alright T, what you doing up? Got a call off Bunny this morning sez you was fucking round there until six?'

'Yea, got in bout two hours ago, had to wait until ten to get beer innit. Haha. Still bollocks'd, kid.'

'Fuck me. Bunny get some in then? You don't look too bad, to be honest.'

'Yea, and the rest. Got fucking twatted mate, proper. It's better than fucking pills innit. Cunt was lobbing plates at the dog, he was that battered. Fuck that. I left. Haha.'

Tyler owed Dode 50 quid from New Year's Eve. He'd got a load of coke in and knew full well he wouldn't pay Dode back. He was fucking Dode's cousin Maz, and couldn't quite understand why

Dode was so chuffed about it. He got the impression Dode looked up to him a bit, plus he never hassled him for the money, so fuck it. He ain't getting it. Dode leaned against the till area.

'One of them Wholenuts too please, duck. You walking up, T?'

'Yea, hold on.'

Tyler put four cans of Foster's on the counter.

'Ten Benson too, please. One of them lighters too, ta.'

The road screamed a flat silence and the pathway battled with the crap grass that threatened it from either side. Mowers hummed in the near distance and the occasional twat in a fast car let rip along the strait that led to the Close.

'How did that court thing go?'

'Put me on some fucking sex offenders register. Fuck's all that about.'

'What does that mean then?'

'Means the cunts are gunna keep an eye on me, don't it.'

'Hardly mate. I think the fucking CID 'ave got better things to do than hang around your street, hahaha. I mean, I'd go insane casing that fucking shed you live in all day, hahaha.'

'Yea, but it's fucking embarrassing innit. I mean I feel really fucking mad about it. I don't understand it.'

'Have ya seen her since then?'

'Fuck off! Coppers said I had to stay clear. She got me fucking banned from the Owl. Can't even fucking remember it to be honest. Fucking coppers going on like I'm a fucking murderer or something.'

They stopped at the turning for the Close.

'Fuck it, mate. It'll blow over.'

'Better do. Lads at work found out. That Scottish crew that joined us last week. All day in me left fucking ear with these jokes about me. By Thursday I thought, 'fuck this' and bunked off. Got pissed in this pub in Barnet, bought some gear off this bloke, some Cockney cunt who was talking to me knew. Had a enough of it, T. Fucking had enough.'

Dode starts scraping his feet on the crap grass, eyes fixed to the floor. Tyler didn't know what to do.

'I'll see you later, mate.'

'See ya in a bit, Dode.'

Tyler walked off up the road struggling to feel convinced about his snap purchase and wondered if four cans of Kronenbourg may have been better.

'Cunt's definitely not getting his money. Fucking pervert.'

Steak Frites

'Why do you buy the fucking things then? They last five fucking minutes. Don't buy the fucking things then. Because I'm not going to make them last, am I? That's absolute bollocks! You just end up eating the fucking things, don't you.'

Rayen put her glass down.

'Well no, you don't actually. No, you don't at all. The idea is to take it easy with them, not fucking hoover them up as soon as the shopping has been delivered. Do you wanna do the fucking shopping in future? Because I'm always fighting you off my phone when I'm ordering the shopping, aren't I? And so what if a group of mums want to have a bottle of champagne at Soft Play, it's a fucking hard job! Why you getting judgmental about it? Is there literally nothing else you can be thinking about?'

'I just thought it was a bit crap, that's all.'

'Why? Because five women were having a drink and not five men?'

'No! Because five women were having a fucking drink in Soft Play with their kids there.'

'Oh my. Have you suddenly been transported back to the 13th century? Are you about to condemn them for being fucking witches?'

Stott pulled himself out of the minor argument and just comically squirmed at Rayen. She looked at him and slapped his arm with the menu before getting up to visit the loo. Stott eyed the woman next to him and looked at her. Did she have facial surgery for the enhancement? Because it clearly didn't look enhanced, it looked fucking awful. Maybe she had it to display the obvious wealth she carried, she looked fucking minted. Perhaps to the financially comfortable or the Rich, plastic surgery was like this kind of trophy cabinet you can attach to your body or face. *It's just another way of wearing Vuitton, isn't it? But in the same breath if it makes people happy then, why not?* All this fucking bias against Rich people, wealthy fuckers, it got on his tits at times because to him very few of these detractors meant it. In his experience most of these fucking lobbyists and self-proclaimed anarchists were just out to blame a 'thing,' any fucking thing. *Pick an object - any object will do!* Or in some cases using it as a vehicle to hide, nurture and eventually hatch timely career moves. Such was, in Stott's mind, the distorted vein of current social critique with its representatives. Perhaps it's always been this way, he thought, each era carries a fair share of bullshitters who appear to the onlooker as people lacing the times with important words. But time isn't stupid. Time denies them credibility and history leaves them where they belong. Time only carries through the real messengers, the true apostles of each mile in civilisation's reign. The vulgarity clearly existed though, you know, that gap and Stott knew it. The Rich appeared in his mind and across his perceptive palate like rotten milk in heat-softened four-pint plastic containers.

He tapped his phone on the table in time with the '90s lounge music coming through the speakers and thought about his own gender. *The men never get it, do they*, the self-loathing began to creep in as he pondered his own conditioning and how he really viewed women when all the fucking virtue signalling had gone. Misogyny was now perceived in 'enlightened' circles as being this kind of crap fire that was slowly dying out and this was dangerous, clearly. Because there is a chance, he thought, that as it was now being widely discussed in the public arena it was starting to appear outwardly as an issue well on the way to being overcome due to the amount of 'enlightened' people talking about it. And so it was as if the war against women was now going the way of historic health issues like polio or the common cold. *Oh yes that thing! Yes, it doesn't bother us anymore! We're over it, you know!* The saving grace of the enlightened carrying the ashes of blanket female hatred to the big hole they've dug out; and there they will bury it forever in an orgy of Likes and Follows. Stott felt pathetic in his below par understanding. The loose bag that he entered the world in still clung to the soles of his shoes.

'What are you having?'

Rayen fell back into her seat.

'The usual.'

'Haha.'

'What?'

'Nothing. Just funny, isn't it. They must put bets on what we are going to order every time we come in.'

'I think they have a bit more to think about other than our sorry arses.'

'Oooer, pointy.'

'Really? I was at the gym yesterday and you know that waiter? The fit one who served us last Saturday?'

'Yea.'

'Well he had massive slash marks going over both his wrists, like fucking really big ones. He must have been through some shit you know.'

'Really?'

'Yea.'

'Fuck.'

'He's nice too, isn't he.'

'Yea.'

'What about thingy then?'

'Who's fucking thingy?'

'Carla.'

'What about her?'

Rayen suddenly catches on.

'Look unfollow her if it's doing your head in. Easy!'

'You can't unfollow people, can you. She'll know, and that's rude innit.'

'How is that rude, you idiot? Honestly. It's fucking social media! You're not exactly going to her fucking house with a hammer in the middle of the night, are you.'

'Yea, I know but …'

'But what? Just flick past her posts then. I mean, to be honest you just like hating on people, don't you, and that's why you keep going on about it.'

'She's shit though, isn't she.'

'Yes, she is shit. I saw her in the park last week and I thought yea, she's fucking basic, but …'

'Well basic.'

'But you know if it makes her happy then why not! Why shouldn't she do it?'

'Because she doesn't do it very well.'

'Well that's your opinion, isn't it, and not the opinion of the people who follow her.'

'Yea, but they don't know shit either. Have you seen some of them? Fucking corpses that cling on to anything. Look, you're right, she does have a right to do whatever makes her happy, of course she does. But the other side of this is how can that be logical when she is actually guilty of stunting Art's growth? I mean, what she's doing is merely replicating tedium, and tedium is the cousin of visionless despair where creative application is destroyed eternally.'

'God, you're a twat at times. A TWAT.'

'It's true though.'

'It's a plausible point, yes, but look around you. We live in the global mediocre village. It's designed to initiate such behaviour and it does that most of the fucking time. It's like that the world over. There are millions of Carlas because life requires that we tow the fucking line, so in a way you should be thanking her, because she's allowing you to be able to think on a supposedly different level through doing what she does. The Equilibrium has been cast if you like. It's like she's almost sacrificed her life for you, ha ha, with your selective fucking nodding and pretentiousness, ha ha. It's like the bin man, isn't it? Some fucker has to do it, don't they.'

'Bin person.'

'Oh, fuck off. Look, Carla's a bit like a spider if you think about it. You get rid of the spiders and the place is infested with millions of other insects, insects that eventually destroy all around you because they don't conform to a pattern as such. The order has gone, hasn't it? Chaos consumes the far corners where once the spider kept them neat and tidy. But that's gone, say. And these invading insects who don't listen to anyone else go round conducting their own arrogant existences which is a bit like you, isn't it, and all the rest of these so-called Artists with these singular ideals dipped in suffering or whatever. You need people like Carla to exist because if she didn't exist where would your reaction come from, smart arse? The world would be infested with too much individual creativity. It would actually destroy the idea of Art, wouldn't it? It would be say like looking at a million different cereal boxes all of the fucking time with their bright colours and bizarre images, et cetera, et cetera. You'd go fucking mad, wouldn't you? A world saturated in real art, a world that resisted and banished commerciality, would be like having a torch pushed into your fucking face 24/7.'

The pain of selection hung heavy in the restaurant. Selection in everything and the people eating had the exhausted look of those who had played the process far too much. The cutthroat world of *Taste* rose above its subjects and formed a sheet of mist at *menu* height. It clung to the inner caves that formed each body and directed them as and when. Shades and shapes and brilliant confidence were like cannon balls at the ready, as each ship sailed in and out of the hot zones where prices where not looked at or considered.

'Sorry, guys. Really busy today. Can I take your order?'

'No worries at all! Steak and Frites please, haha.'

'Ah! Of course! I should of known, ha ha. Medium for you, sir?'

'Please.'

'And rare for you?'

'Thank you.'

'Sparkling and Still?'

'Yes, please.'

Rayen eyed the waiter as he walked off.

'He's fit, eh?'

'Good looking bloke, yea. Lives in Wipple Park though.'

'No! It's a shithole there.'

'Well, I guess he's not earning much here, is he.'

'How do you know anyway?'

'Saw him last week in Boots.'

'Fit though.'

'OK easy, fucking hell.'

'Hahaha.'

'So ,Wood Road ...'

'850 it's up for, eight fucking 50.'

'I know. He won't get that though, no way. Eight, I reckon.'

'He's done it well though, looks nice. Not seen the interior, mind.'

'Exactly. I mean the driveway is basic. Come on, it's pretty shit, those bricks are cheap too.'

'Big place though, and my guess is that inside is gunna be just 'OK.' Like fucking twee or something, so you know it's gunna appeal to a lot of people, isn't it.'

'What? Like Carla? Haha.'

'Thing is, the guy was told in like fucking Feb or something that he'd only get four for it and to not bother doing anything to it either, because he'd be wasting his money.'

'Crazy.'

'Yep.'

'That coach house too.'

Oh God, yea. Did you see it on Right Move? Fuck. It's tiny! No wonder she always ignores us, hahaha.'

'Did you not think to say hello to her?'

'No, she looks unapproachable.'

'Fuck off.'

Time passes.

'Hello! OK, medium steak for you, sir, and the rare for you, madam ...'

'Thank you.'

'And your Sparkling and Still.'

'Thank you.'

'Can I get you anything else?'

'French mustard, please.'

'Certainly.'

It was like admiring the shape of your calves as two people were forcing somebody else into an industrial shredder only a few yards away from you. The A Side/B Side; 'Terror' and its flipside 'Possessions and Serenity.' But the nervousness, the fragile state in which consciousness held the burden of such a reality, balanced like a ton weight on top of a fly's skull. If you walked two metres to the left you were tortured to death with a blowtorch and fork. Two metres to the right and you were having your chest size measured in Gucci. The oiled bodies of decent porn stars acted as DNA that ran through a toilet pipe at the back of Nero's. The rules of attraction were this: 'I like you, fuck me. I don't care about anything really, check my chilled vibe.' A maze appeared before you but not in a 'Life is a Test' type fucking way; just a senseless undoable mess of direction that ate your legs if you didn't move and laughed at you if you got Cancer again. The streets were pristine library rows and occasionally you would feel the onset of a panic attack if you spotted someone walking towards you who you knew. The effort to actually conjure up conversation became a bigger ordeal than anything ever.

You would turn the other way or do anything, absolutely anything, to disconnect from the head-on collision. The laws fell on your face like an adult human body dropped from 50 feet. It dragged you into a wall of death as you sloped around its desirable streets uttering various aspects from its injection into your mind.

Stott dipped his last frite in the French mustard and put it into his mouth where at the back, in the left hand corner, his last piece of minute steak lay waiting to be amalgamated and dropped into the folds of digestion.

'Can you stop looking at that waiter guy, please?'

'Are you getting jealous? Haha. Oh, come on. As if.'

'What are you having for dessert, you big tart?'

'I'm not. Fuck sugar. You?'

'I'm going with the cheese.'

'You checked them out first? They FOD smart?'

'Oh, fuck it. I'm having a day off.'

'Don't come running to me then when you're having to stand in the corner of the kitchen every five minutes because your arse is pouring out Satan's Horlicks.'

Dolled Up

'Get them pink ones,' Bod pointed over. 'Them ones there, now!'

'Is he looking?'

'Yea. Fuck me, he's looking, alright! Pulling a right fucking face. Hahahahaha.'

'Hahahahahaha, jokin!'

'I'm not. Now get that navy thong and hold it up as if ya examining it.'

Gyp held the pink heels in one hand and the navy knickers in the other, whilst Bod tried not to look as if he was watching the bloke and his partner who were staring at them at the other end of the aisle.

'He looks fucking disgusted.'

'Jokin?'

'No. Seriously. Put them in the basket, fuck it. Let's go for it now.'

'Now? We've only just got here.'

'I reckon he's ripe. He looks like a thick cunt. He looks ripe. His missus too. Let's head for the tills and see what happens.'

The expressionless cashier put both items through quicker than a sneeze. He looked at them both.

'Any cashback?'

'No ta, mate.'

The supermarket was pretty full, but much to Bod and Gyp's dismay it was mostly elderly folk until, of course, they stumbled across two younger people as they headed down the underwear aisle. From then on it was proper gravy.

'Fuck me, that couple are paying, mate. Good hunch.'

'Where?'

'Three aisles up. He's looking at us, too.'

'OK. Let's head to the magazine and newspaper bit near the entrance. Make out we're buying fags, waste some time. Shout me when they are near us.'

'OK.'

Bod sloped onto the main walkway with the bag in his hand passing the ends of each chromed till station as Gyp followed him. They took it slow.

'They're behind us, mate.'

'OK, let's head to the entrance.'

'Ya not getting fags?'

'Fuck that, get em later.'

The car park was busy. It had to be really. It was important they hit places that held a high percentage of probability. Supermarkets were a good bet, Friday afternoons being the best option. Either that, or say Sunday mid morning before the pubs filled up and the ovens were turned on, or whenever payday hit each month. The early evening glow from a descending sun hit Bod's face as he scoped the skyline's beauty, plane trails across the rich blue sheet.

'Oi!'

The bloke and his partner were pretty close to them, their pace quickened. The twat bellowed again.

'Oi!!!'

Bod kept walking but Gyp stopped and turned round.

'You talking to us?'

Bod now stopped walking too.

The man became enraged instantly. He pounded up to them and halted about two metres away, whilst his partner stood slightly behind.

'Yea, I fucking am. You gunna wear that shit then, you gay cunt?'

Bod smashed him in the face with his left fist, dropped the bag and then followed through with his right. The bloke staggered, shocked. Bod then repeated the process, whilst Gyp pursued his partner who had shot round the back of her fella to get to Bod. Gyp threw her into the side of a line of empty trollies and punched her in the mouth. She kinda rolled along the line of trollies for a few seconds and then crashed to the floor, screaming with rage:

'YOU FUCKING QUEER CUNT. YOU FUCKING CUNT. YOU ARE FUCKING DEAD, YOU FAGGOT CUNT.'

Gyp took a run up and kicked her right in the face. She whacked the back of her head on the walkway and then screamed a sound that he had never heard in all his days. He didn't follow through with anything else, the four teeth scattered on the floor made him stop. Bod was now intensely stamping on the bloke's face as he lay out on the walkway. The fight wasn't going the *multiphobe's* way. The shock had permanently weakened any counterattack. His partner had now managed to get on all her fours as a stream of vomit biblically hurled itself from her mouth, spraying sections of the lined and empty trollies pressing against the wall that led to the supermarket's entrance. It was a good one.

The sun carded through the bottom of Bod's bedroom window as he tried to sleep some more, but the scrapes of the radio in the kitchen, spitting noises like the empty response to a desperate SOS call, wouldn't let him. He swung out of bed, slipped out of his room and into the kitchen.

'Mum, for fuck's sake, can't you tune this thing?'

Bod's mum Lynne was sat on the step of the back door that opened into the kitchen, smoking and jabbing letters into her phone.

'Sorry, duck. Didn't even notice. I just switch it on of a morning don't er. Haha. Tea in the pot, if you want it. Still hot.'

'Any coffee?'

'Yea, if you make it. I forgot to buy the special stuff, you know.'

'What special stuff?'

'The stuff that can make it's fucking self, ya know. Haha.'

Bod churned a coffee out and sat in the living room. He drank two cups and rolled a fag, the nicotine ambushing any natural bodily reaction to the new day. He slumped for a few minutes.

'Mum? You seen my phone?'

The English Host was a large building. It had always been a pub but it didn't look like one. It looked like an old '70s business block. The only giveaways were the large brass letters going from one end of the building to the other, and the rectangular windows that also lined each section at the front of the building. On a hot day these were flung open as drinkers sat at the ends of the tables.

Gyp parked the car directly outside the Host. Bod was in the passenger seat. It was just past 2pm and the sun was beating against the pub's walls. Drinkers filled each window as the Isley Brothers' 'This Old Heart Of Mine' carried through. Bod got out the car in black hot pants, yellow heels and a charcoal blouse that finished just above his belly button. He walked to the end of the car and opened the boot, bending right the way in to retrieve a green suede holdall. It took 18 seconds before two lads from the window nearest the car walked out on the pavement. One of them piped up instantly.

'I don't think anybody ordered an ugly stripper, you bent cunt. What the fuck are you wearing?'

Gyp got out the driver's side in nothing but light blue French knickers and corked platforms with black velvet straps. One more bloke from the same table stepped onto the pavement. Gyp walked around the front of the car. He opened the passenger door and removed a brick from the footwell. The additional multiphobe joined the other two, who had by now reached the far corner of the car as Bod stood there fumbling with the bag.

'I'm not a stripper, mate. Where did you get that idea, then?'

The leading bloke's eyes stiffened.

'I don't get ideas when it comes to cunts like you. Do you understand me, bum boy? I don't get ideas because I already know what to do, do y …'

Before he could finish his sentence Gyp had moved from behind Bod and smashed the corner of the brick into the bloke's eye socket. The bloke didn't move back however, he was solid. Gyp's move only served to set him off like a packet of fat fucking fireworks. He tried to grab at the brick that Gyp was planning to land into his face for a second time but Gyp let go and, before the bloke could get a firm hold, Bod pulled out a small nail hammer from the holdall and sank its claw end into the bloke's lower neck muscle. The other bloke behind the first moved in sharpish but Bod threw the hammer into the boot quickly, then swung and punched the first guy (who was by now bleeding very badly) in the left ear, so as to clear the way.

Bod grabbed at the second bloke's head. He pulled him in closer and bit into his left cheek. The man let out a sharp scream. The third man hurried around the front of the car so as to come from behind Bod and Gyp, but Gyp clocked him. Gyp grabbed the hammer that lay at the front of the boot and swung the claw end into the side of the bloke's chest just below his rib cage. Another scream, and this caused the onset of panic amongst the Host's spectators. Nobody else joined in. Bod had still got his teeth into the second bloke's face as the man tried to pull him off, but couldn't. The screams were deeply unsettling as they both squirmed in a rotational pattern on the floor. Bod stuck to his face like an animal.

The first guy lay wounded on the floor as Gyp, bending over him, battered his throat with the small rounded hammer head. No one helped. No coppers turned up. Gyp dropped the hammer, jumped over the first bloke, skirting around the heaped mess that was Bod and his man, to take care of the third multiphobe who had by now managed to get back onto the pathway and towards the table he sprang from. Gyp calmly walked over to the driver's door, opened it and pulled a pencil out from the drinks hole near the gearstick. He marched at the bloke, who had now suddenly changed his mind and decided to move in on Gyp by going for his waist with his arms, but Gyp just drove the pencil into the guy's lower back. The bloke screamed again, folding like a shit DIY table with too many tools on its deck. Gyp pulled the pencil out and paused for a moment. It suddenly dawned on him that the congregated mass of spectating pub warts were now getting restless. The fear was turning into anger.

'Let's go, mate.'

Bod got up instantly, retrieved the hammer, slammed the car boot and got into the passenger side.

'Thing is, your body isn't like anybody else's, is it?'

They were parked in a field about four miles out of town. It was a while after the attack at the Host. Gyp drew on a roll up, flicked the ash out of the window followed by a mouth full of spit.

'What do you mean?'

'Well you know, you could work out every day, say five hours a day. All the exercises and that, but your body would still look different to those fuckers in magazines.'

'Course it wouldn't, you twat.'

'Course it would! These blokes in the magazines are fucking airbrushed and all that shit. Plus, they are on these fucking expensive diets and that.'

Gyp took another drag and flicked the rest of the roll up out the window.

'Nah. I can't see it, to be honest. You're gunna look the same. Course you are.'

'Go on then, prove me wrong. Get down that gym for the next, say, year or something.'

Gyp looked at Bod.

'Fuck that. Three times a week is enough. No shit food if I can help it. I don't wanna look like I've got my intestines on display, you know. That's just too much. Sure, if ya into that kind of thing on a competition level, but normal day-to-day, looking like that? Nah, looks too much.'

The Seeping Oak was a bar in the Glade district situated across the river from the main town centre. Dated house music would pulsate on a Thursday, Friday and Saturday to busy crowds. In the week it played host to crap food and cheesy singer/songwriters scratching out horrible versions of classic songs. Bod watched the bouncer of the Oak stand in the middle of the path as the place filled up. There was no need for him to be obstructing the pathway as he was. Bod hated the cunt. He looked like Steve Strange on sausages, the cunt. These fucking muscle boys intimidating the punters as they walked in to spend their hard earned money, money that was paying his fucking wages. The bouncer's name was Paul Clear. Bod had made some enquiries and prepared accordingly. Paul was a cokehead, he drank a lot and, through a source Bod knew from the gym, took steroids frequently. Bod got out the car in a long pink champagne dress tight to the bone. He wore dark navy heels with straps, which looked a bit odd but these particular shoes made his legs look great. As normal, he would wear no make-up, no hairstyle, to complement the outfit. He walked over the car park towards the ticket machine and paid for 30 minutes worth of parking.

Inside the Oak, Gyp was leaned against the bar in regular clothing. Bod walked back to his car, opened the door and placed the car parking ticket on the dashboard. He then pulled out a small evening bag, locked the car and walked towards the Oak. Paul eyed Bod from the zebra crossing opposite the Oak, and watched him cross and walk in. Bod said nothing, he didn't look at Paul, who also remained quiet. The bar wasn't too busy, but as Bod approached somebody pinched his arse. He turned round and three blokes were smirking at their pints.

'Was that you, mate?'

The bloke nearest Bod looked up.

'Mate? I'm not your mate, sweetness.'

Bod moved in closer and whispered:

'You talk to me like that again, you thick cunt and I will fuck your dead mum in front of you. Do you understand?'

The bloke's mouth dropped and his posture froze. Gyp moved in behind Bod.

'Oi lads. Leave him, will ya. Let's not fall out.'

'Let's not fall out? Bum boy just said he was going to fuck my mum.'

Gyp pulled out a concealed carrot peeler and gave it to Bod, who in turn lurched at the bloke and grabbed him by the back of the head. Bod then proceeded to smash the bloke's teeth in with the peeler as Gyp threw his pint at the other two men, before landing multiple punches on them both. Paul ran in from the entrance and jumped straight onto Bod. Bod and Paul fell to the floor. The two men being attacked by Gyp scurried back desperately as Gyp now started jumping on their legs as and when he could. Bod and Paul fought for upmanship as Gyp turned around and grabbed Paul's hair from the top. He dragged Paul back slightly so as to free Bod's arms a little. Bod pulled his arms out from the tangle, retrieved the carrot peeler on the floor next to him and buried it deep into the side of Paul's mouth. Paul screamed, but not for long. Gyp started jumping on his head as Bod started stabbing the carrot peeler into Paul's chest. It was over for Paul. Nobody helped. No coppers turned up. It was a good one.

AS